T0113309

INTERNATIONAL CONSPIRACY

Charles Roebuck

authorHOUSE®

AuthorHouse™
1663 Liberty Drive
Bloomington, IN 47403
www.authorhouse.com
Phone: 1 (800) 839-8640

© 2016 Charles Roebuck. All rights reserved.

No part of this book may be reproduced, stored in a retrieval system, or transmitted by any means without the written permission of the author.

Published by AuthorHouse 10/13/2016

ISBN: 978-1-5246-4507-6 (sc)
ISBN: 978-1-5246-4506-9 (e)

Print information available on the last page.

Any people depicted in stock imagery provided by Thinkstock are models, and such images are being used for illustrative purposes only. Certain stock imagery © Thinkstock.

This book is printed on acid-free paper.

Because of the dynamic nature of the Internet, any web addresses or links contained in this book may have changed since publication and may no longer be valid. The views expressed in this work are solely those of the author and do not necessarily reflect the views of the publisher, and the publisher hereby disclaims any responsibility for them.

Germany

August 29, 1939

Hitler smashed the coal of his cigar into his gloved left hand as he stood on the steps of The Berghof. In disdain he watched as the silver and black limo, accompanied by four armed men on motorcycles pulled up and stopped in front of him. The young guard opened the rear door and four men exited the vehicle, then saluted their Furher and walked up the steps to the main entrance. They hung their coats in the foyer, then proceeded through the villas main room then out on the viranda where the servants had made preparations for lunch. His guests included Reinhard Heydrich, Chief of security for the S.S, Heinrich Himmler, head of the Propaganda Ministry, Adolph Eichmann, head of Jewish Affairs and finally Heinrich Muller, Chief of Riech Security.

"Have some drinks" the Furher said as he entered the viranda and instructed his men to be seated.

They gathered their cocktails and took their seats at the long rectangular table which was oiled high with luncheon meats, breads, salads and desserts. They dressed their sandwiches and piled their plates with food, ate and did by no later than November. The plan for the Final Solution would be ready to move forward and then the rest of Europe would have little resistance to the German war machine.

The men stayed up till the early morning hours with some of the local woman. They drank and sang songs dedicated to the Third Reich, to the pure people of their country and to the future.

The next day after breakfast Hitler and his men were extremely pleased as they laughed and joked on the way to their limo. Der Furher was excited as well, almost giddy at the fact that his plan was finally coming together. He embraced his men and patted them on the back as they each climbed into the vehicle.

It was a new day for Germany. He and its people would have their wish to have a Jew free world and create a legacy that would go on for many, many generations.

And so it begins.

8:00AM

Present Day

The November morning was brisk he thought as he got dressed and headed to the coffee shop on Duval Street for some caffeine and the morning paper. The Southern Most city's main drag in Old Town boasted fourteen blocks of Spanish style buildings and was the center of attraction for this historic town. Full of pastel colored shops, quaint eateries, and a large amount of bars, Key West offered a magical lure for people all over the world. It was paradise for the thousands who embraced the beauty of the ocean and watched in awe as the sun set, then reveled in debauchery to an endless amount of night time activities.

This time of the day, the street was fairly deserted and the wind was unusually strong as he walked the four blocks to the coffee shop. Island living was modest and the people you see got to know your daily habits and as he walked into the coffee shop his order was ready before he approched the counter. He gave the girl a five, grabbed a paper and told the girl to keep the change. She smiled, maybe even blushed, thanked him and said she would come down to his bar for a cocktail. Jake told her he looked forward to it and offered to get her first round, walked out the door and headed back to his house. It wasn't that the girl was cute or even attractive but it was the fact that he always insisted on treating people the way that they wanted to be treated.

Always a stand-up guy, Jake Jones was born in Carbondale, Illinois to the son of a Baptist minister. He left for Key West in 1995, never looked back and never missed snow. His folks visited often and admired the fact that he'd found paradise. They knew it was his chance to live his dream of fishing and diving and when they come to visit he'd treat them to the same experiences that he had. All the Jones' wanted for their son was to be happy and if fishing, bartending and boozing was what made him happy, then so were they.

Over the years Jake had reinvented himself into a locals favorite, and after having many meaningless jobs on the Island, working at the Tiki bar made him a hit not only with the locals, the tourists were infatuated with him as well. The girls threw themselves at him, but at the end of the day he was devoted to Lisa, his girl of five years. She was his everything and couldn't picture a day in paradise without her.

His love of five years was back sleeping at the house and wouldn't be awake until mid morning so he decided to take a walk down to the Schooner Wharf Bar on Lazy Way about two blocks away. The locals called it the breakfast club and the place appealed to all kinds of people, drunks, cabbies, hotel staff and vacationers pulling an all night bender. If you could stand the roaches, the rats and the stench of the place, Schooner was a fun hangout. It brought out old Key West and the way the Island used to be, when it was a seaman's paradise.

He walked toward the bar and weaved through a half dozen drunken people swaying to a Jimmy Buffet cover tune, and sat down on a stool facing the water. The bartender put a Bloody Mary down on the bar, wished him a good morning and went back to working his crowd. He swiveled the bar stool around towards the water. The view was captivating even though the water was choppy from the wind but looked like a good day for sailing, he thought.

His phone in his front pocket was ringing. He took it out and looked at it. It was his friend, Jonathan, a cab driver at night and suspected hacker by day. It was odd Jake thought he would call this early in the morning. The man got done with his shift at 6am and was usually in bed by now. What the hell, he might be in jail he thought, so he answered it.

"What's up man, you in jail" Jake asked laughing?

"I got to meet with you now, I got something for you. Where you at?" Jonathan asked.

"I'm at Schooner for a quick drink, Lisa won't be up for a while. "I got a few minutes to kill" Jake said as he sensed a little disparity in his voice.

"Alright man, I need you to hold something for me, Ok" he said.

"I'll be here for another twenty minutes" Jake said.

"Be there in fifteen" Jonathan replied.

Jake sat there looking at the catamarans. He and Jonathan had been friends for many years an trusted the guy more than he trusted any of his relatives and if the man wanted him to hold something, he'd be there for him and it was nt unusual for someone to be in a little trouble in the Key's

The tall ships were getting ready for their daily tours and snorkel trips when a young girl sporting a T shirt that said "I heart Key West" walked up to the bar. He looked over at the girl who couldn't have been more than fourteen. She was holding a small envelope in both of her hands. The bartender said a few words to her and pointed in Jakes direction and she walked over to him.

"Is your name Jake, because this guy came up to me in this T-shirt shop down the street and gave me twenty dollars to give this too you" She said as she chewed a mouthful of gum.

"What man?" He asked.

"Don't know. He had long greasy hair and he seemed like he was in a hurry. I usually wouldn't do this kinda stuff but I can buy a few more T-shirts for my friends back home. There's nothing bad in there is there mister? She said.

He thanked her as he took the envelope from her and reassured her that everything was fine and wished her a good vacation as she went down the water walk. Looking in the envelope, there was a flash-drive in it. He scanned the bar to see if anything was unusual or anyone was watching, but didn't notice anything out of the ordinary.

Jonathan was always enigmatic but this was a little more than usual. Once in a while he would come to his bar and hand him some disks with pirated movies but he was always discreet about handing them to him in private. He understood the penalty for ripping movies off the internet, especially when they hadn't even been released to the general public, but sending a total stranger to give him a flash drive, that was too cloak and dagger. What was more strange, was what he heard after he speed dialed Jonathans phone, a recording that said the number he had reached was no longer in service.

He felt that there was something wrong.

8:45AM

He tried several other numbers. Either everyone was sleeping or to hung over to answer the phone. He decided to call the cab company and find out what was going on. Maybe they would be able to get in touch with him since he did computer work on the side for the company. The girl picked up the phone and told him that they hadn't seen or heard from him in three days and if he'd ever hear from Jonathan again, to tell him he was fired.

Jake took the last sip of the Bloody Mary and looked around at the ten customers sitting at the bar to see if he recognized anyone. There was a guy who had an argument with his girl at his bar the previous night, but didn't recognise anybody else. He got up and headed for the exit when a man with bloodshot eyes leaned over to say something to him but fell off the stool, face first into the sand. He'd seen enough of the Schooner Bar and the best thing to do was not talk to anyone and get the flash-drive back to the house. He removed it from the envelope and put it in the front pocket of his cargo shorts and left towards Caroline Street, through the rear exit.

The walk home was brisk and the wind started to pick up as he turned left on Simonton Street. He looked over his shoulder frequently but didn't think he ws being followed. He thought about Jonathan as he crossed over Eaton Street. Maybe he was on a bender or had his phone disconnected from lack of payment. Or, he was holed up at a bar called Billie's on Front Street shooting the shit with Pat the bartender. If a locals wanted to disappear, Billie's Bar was the perfect place. It was mostly a local crowd full of shady people, where very few tourists ventured into its dark hole.

It took Jake twelve minutes to get home to 808 Simonton Street. It was his sanctuary from the hustle and bustle of work and his work was stressful being a bartender for obnoxious rich people at a five star resort and a Tiki Bar that was constantly busy. If he had two day's off in a row, practically no one would see him out of his palace where he lived in a spacious three bedroom apartment that resembled a small New York style loft, only at half the price. It was a rare upstairs find in Key West, with a huge kitchen and an awesome front porch that overlooked the street which made it fun to people watch in the calm of the night. The rent was right for him and Lisa, at twelve hundred a month and split two ways it freed up a lot of money to have dinner parties on a regular basis with some of his closest friends.

From the outside of the four plex the place looked like it was ready to fall down and the paint peeling facade gave it a real Key West historic look. Originally, It had been a funeral home back in the late 1800's, and as you went up the narrow cracked and broken steps it felt as if you would fall through and perish on the cement below. However, when entering his place, it was equally decorated in a masculine and feminine way with candles, photos of Key West and neutral colors of both of their tastes. The kitchen area truly was his pride and joy and cooking was more to him than just a hobby and it was totally off limits to Lisa and guests. It was an area of the house that brought relaxation and a piece of mind while perfecting his culanary skills that any top chef would admire.

Twenty minutes had passed since he arrived home. The door to the bedroom was still closed which meant Lisa would not going to be awake for a least another hour. He took the flash-drive out of his pocket and looked at it. He noticed it said one-hundred terabytes on it. He had no idea they made a flash-drive that stored that much information. Maybe Jonathan was giving him more movies but he usually got one or two a month he thought as he went to the door to wake Lisa up and to tell her about the bizarre morning that he had down at Schooner Wharf.

He reached the door to the bedroom but there was a knock at the back door. He turned around and saw a shadow on the steps and walked towards the door, but stopped as he was about to open it and slipped the flash-drive in between some magazines. It was way too early to have guests he thought as he yelled out to the person to wait a minute and a male voice replied to him to take his time. He opened the door and was shocked to see that it was the man from Schooner that had argued with his girlfriend the night before. He looked disheveled and possibly drunk so Jake went out on the porch to see why some stranger had followed him to his home.

"Hey what's up buddy, sorry to follow you home" the man said.

"Damn right you're sorry, I really don't have time for this" Jake said.

"I just thought that with the little bit of bonding we had last night after the fight I had with my girl. I just wanted to come and thank you" He said in a slurred speech.

"I don't think this is appropriate to follow people to their homes. Glad I could help, now have a good day" Jake said.

"No man, wait a minute I thought that, You know, at Schooner Wharf" He said almost falling over the rail.

"Like I said buddy your welcome, but this is really inappropriate following me home like this" Jakes aid.

"My girl, she left me YOU KNOW...." he said in an angry tone.

"I'm sorry but I'm not a marriage counselor" Jake told the man as he started to close the door.

Jake was stunned as the man pushed the door open and hit him in the jaw, falling back into the apartment and crashing to the floor. He was dazed as the man picked him up off the floor and threw him into the kitchen. The man hovered over him and pointed a gun with a silencer at him. Jake tried to get onto his feet but the man kicked him back to the floor and demanded something that surprised him.

"I tried to be nice but that isn't working. Where is that fucking flash-drive" he asked?

Jake was taken aback by the question and didn't know what to say as the man stood over him with a mad look in his eyes. The door to the bedroom opened and Lisa ran out to see what the trouble was and as the man reeled around and pointed the gun at her, Jake jumped to his feet and grabbed a meat cleaver off the counter and chopped the man in the back of the head at the base of his skull and spine. He fell to the floor squeezing off three rounds as he hit with a thud. Lisa dived out of the way behind the sofa screaming. He knew the man was dead but kicked the gun away and ran over to her wher she was lying in a fetal position, crying hysterically

"Are you hurt baby? Have you been shot?" He asked.

She was hysterical and wouldn't calm down so he grabbed her by the face and asked her the same question. She began to calm down but couldn't get any words out. He looked over her body and found she had no holes in her and reassured her that everything was ok.

"Jake, who the hell was that?" she stuttered.

"I don't know but we got to get the hell out of here because it's not safe. You need to get dressed fast. I'll tell you what happened to me this morning. We gotta go Now" he said sternly.

"Did you get into a fight with this man?" She asked

He didn't even say a word he just looked at her and she stood up, but stopped for a second and looked at the pool of blood pouring onto the floor and ran into the bedroom. While she got her clothes on Jake went over to the man and rolled him over and looked for his wallet. No I.D and no wallet. He grabbed the flash-drive from under the magazine, a tee shirt his cell phone and put them into a back pack and both headed for the front door but Jake stopped and picked up the dead mans gun.

"Don't touch that thing, leave it here" she said.

"Hang on babe we're going to need it, there might be more of them" Jake replied.

"More of them. Who are they?" She asked?

9:36AM

Jake looked at the gun in his hand and shoved it into the backpack. They got to the doorway and stopped. He looked at Lisa and put his finger over his lips telling her to be quiet and listen. He knew the third step down from the top creaked and if anyone was coming up, it would be the giveaway. He turned to Lisa and told her that whatever happens not to scream and that everything will be ok.

He poked his head around the corner and didn't see anyone and bolted out the door with Lisa in tow, running down the steps and stopping at the bottom. Jake looked around but didn't see anyone but as he turned around to get to his scooter that was parked in the ally, they were startled by another man holding a gun. He didn't hesitate when the man started to speak he just closed his eyes and squeezed off three rounds through the backpack hitting him in the neck, shoulder and just above the right eyebrow. Blood squirted out of the wound like a fountain as the man fell to the ground. Lisa covered her mouth and looked away from the dying man as she climbed over him to get to the scooter. He lifted up the seat and put the backpack in the storage compartment, started the engine and sped off through the ally behind his apartment.

They raced down the highly vegetative cobblestone pathway and turned left onto Center Street, and hauled ass towards Truman Avenue. Lisa was babbling and repeatedly saying that she couldn't believe what was happening. Jake couldn't either could as he frantically looked behind them looking to see if anyone was following them. They turned right onto Truman Avenue, crossing Duval and Whitehead, and then turning right onto Thomas Street.

"What the hell is going and where are we going, the police station is the other way" she said hysterically.

"We're going to the fort. I need to think for a minute and come up with a plan so I can figure out what the hell is going on. We'll be there in two minutes. Ok" Jake replied

"The Fort, we don't need to go to the fort, we need to go to the cops. Those men tried to kill us" she said.

They turned left onto Southard Street and pulled up to the guard shack and gave the park ranger two dollars to get into Fort Zachary Taylor State Park where a massive Civil War era fort was constructed in 1845 and completed in 1866. It was a huge historic monument with multiple tunnels and passages. Two sides of the structure faced the Gulf and the Atlantic the other sides North and West parts of the island. It was built in the center of 85 acres with sandy beaches behind them which meant that any threat to them would come from only two directions. Strategically, it was a good place to regroup, make a few phone calls and figure out who these people were.

He knew the gift shop manager and the Fort was empty so they parked behind a storage shed in the rear and hopped the yellow rope that led past the army Barracks. No one was inside so they crossed the courtyard and went into the west tunnel far in the back where they wouldn't be seen. He looked behind to see if anyone was following before they went in. It seemed safe, but then he thought about the man in the ally, turned around and stood by the tunnel for a minute. It was all clear for the moment.

They ran towards the far corner cannon station and Lisa grabbed him and started to shake him asking him what had just happened. He sat her down and began to tell her the whole story of the mornings bizarre events. About how Jonathan called him and wanted to meet at Schooner and that he sounded a little strange on the phone, but he insisted on giving him a mysterious flash-drive. He took it from the bag and showed it to her and explained to her that's what the two men were looking for. She asked him why they couldn't just go to the police and he told her that what ever was on the flash-drive had to be so important that even if they gave it to them, they would probably be killed anyway.

"I just can't believe this, we need to tell someone what happened, tell anyone, Jake. Anyone that could help" she said.

"I know, but first we need to collect ourselves. It's not every day that someone tries to kill us" he told her as he touched her face.

He sat down next to her and looked at her. Her eyes welled with tears and he held her as she began to cry. She asked him why Jonathan would give HIM the the flash drive. He had no response except that he told her that Jonathan was one of the best hackers he knew of and that he ripped all of his movies from hacking into the Academy Awards server and pirated them right from the source. He stole movies that hadn't even been released in theaters yet.

He told her Jonathan tried explaining the process to him in the past, but not being too tech inclined it was way too much technical talk for him to understand.

"But whatever we do, we got to do it fast. They'll be looking for us. Especially with two dead guys at our apartment. We need to split up, if we're together they'll hurt both of us. We're around the corner from Steves house. Let's take the scooter and I'll drop you off there. I'll go see Ed at his shop and he'll be able to tell us what's on this flash-drive" he said.

She pleaded with him not to separate but he reassured her that this was the best thing and that he wouldn't get hurt. Whatever had to be on the flash-drive was so important that, whoever wanted it, would try and kill an innocent couple. Ed was the only one that could help him figure out what to do.

Inside the backpack his cell phone started ringing. He took it out and looked at the caller Id. It was Jen, a friend of his for many years and someone he could trust. He answered it. She was sobbing and she began to tell him that someone found Jonathans body at the end of Simonton Street and that he had killed himself. He had shot himself in the head.

"Wholly shit, how did you hear" he asked?

"I got to call from a friend down at the newspaper. He went down to the scene to report on it after he heard it on the scanner. Where are you at" she asked?

"Never mind that, have you been by my place this morning" he asked?

"I was there ten minutes ago and your front door was wide open. I wanted to tell you about Jonathan in person.

They got the end of your street blocked off and the crime scene unit down there" she said.

"You didn't see anything at my place did you" he asked?

"No, just that the door was open. I went inside but I thought you guys were asleep and didn't want to wake you" She said.

"I gotta go, call you back in a minute" He said as he looked over at Lisa and hung up the phone.

"What's wrong" she asked?

"It was Jen, she said that they found Jonathans body at the end of our street. He shot himself. And, she was at our place and didn't see any of the dead guys" he said.

He was dead and there was nothing that they could do. Lisa got up off the ground and he grabbed her hand and walked towards the way they came in. As they turned the corner Jake froze as a big black Hummer pulled onto the courtyard across from the barracks. They backed off and went back inside. Four men dressed in Army fatigues carrying assault rifles exited the Hummer. Jake could hardly hear what they were saying but had a clue what they were going to do next.

The men were branching out, heading towards different parts of the fort. They had nowhere to go but then, Jake remembered something an old friend had showed him a few years back. He turned around and dragged Lisa by the arm thirty yards down the corridor turning left into a dead end.

"Where are we going? Those guys are going to kill us aren't they?" she asked.

"Not if I can help it" he replied.

He had remembered something that maybe three people on the island knew about. In front of him it looked like just an average gunner station with a small square opening to point a musket barrel out of, but as he turned to his right he grabbed a large steel ring, pulled on it then pushed with his shoulder on the brick wall and it opened two feet.

He could hear the men running down the cobblestone floor in each direction. Their combat boots echoed off the thick brick walls. Lisa didn't hesitate to enter the opening and Jake followed behind her. Once inside, he put his back into the brick door and shoved it closed.

It was pitch black inside. Lisa started to speak and Jake whispered to her to be quiet. He heard the men stop. They were talking outside the hidden doorway. The walls were a foot thick and he couldn't make out what they were saying but sensed they were angry. Even after all that has happened in the past few hours, Jake still managed to laugh at the irony of the situation.

The tunnel was musty. The smell of old dirt was overpowering as Jake fished through the backpack and came across a small squeezable flashlight that his hotel gave to its guests as small tokens of appreciation. He had always thought that they were cheesy gifts to give when the average person was spending three to five thousand for a weeks' vacation in paradise. Up until today he never really used one but today it was the best thing he ever kept in the small back-pack.

He squeezed the small flashlight and Lisa's face lit up. She was standing two feet in front of him and managed to smiled at him and for a second all he could think about was that there was no way in Hell anything was going to happen to her because he loved her so much and right now.

Her safety was all that mattered. He leaned over and kissed her soft lips.

"I told you I wouldn't let anything happen to you, right" he said.

"You did Jake, but where does this go and how did you know about it" she asked?

"The curator and historian of the fort" He and I got drunk one night and came down here. He told me he had found some old schematics of the fort from a hundred years ago and noticed in this small little area that something didn't look right. We came over here and did a little investigating and discovered this tunnel on accident. It was years ago that we came here and showed it to me but I had forgotten about it until now" he said.

"I think we really lucked out" she said.

"I don't know about luck, but maybe there was some reason for coming here" he said.

He explained to her that the curator had done some research and talked with one of the oldest historians on the island and found out that the tunnel had been built for President Taylor as a secret exit in case the fort had been overthrown by the Confederate army. Unfortunately Taylor died before he could ever visit the fort and over time, it had been forgotten about, even lost in the modern blueprints of the fort.

****

"Sir, we looked over the whole area, the scooter is here but they're nowhere to be found. What are your orders Commander" The soldier asked as he ran up to the black Hummer.

"Ops, Sinclair here, I need blueprints of Fort Taylor ASAP and get air support off their asses. The subjects have slipped through and send six more units to secure a half mile radius from the southernmost point to the court house. No military uniforms, low key only. And get me a God damn boat out on the water" Sinclair said as he flipped his phone closed and turned to the Sergeant.

"Commander the subjects couldn't have gotten far. My units have it under control" Sgt. Taylor said.

"Taylor you don't have shit under control. What the hell was that crap on Simonton Street. I have two agents and a hacker dead. Your men were supposed to get the flash drive and leave. What the hell happened Sergeant" Sinclair said as he stepped into his face.

"We didn't have confirmation on the drop sir; we thought Pressley would show up at Schooner Bar after his last phone call. We had the men in place but he sent a young girl to make the drop but the agents weren't sure if Jones had them" Taylor responded.

"So your men, two Navy Seals get killed in the process. This simple job that your men screwed up is going to cost us with the local authorities. Get me more information on this bartender and keep your men under control Sergeant, I don't want any more killing. None, you understand Sergeant" Commander Sinclair said as he climbed into the Hummer and looked at the laptop mounted to the dashboard.

"Yes Sir" Sgt. Taylor said. "Everyone regroup. Our subjects are not here, they slipped away. Private, head to the guard shack. You two sweep out over the old Navy property and check the old barracks to the north. We got units rolling in to cover the streets from the southernmost point to the

courthouse. Use non-lethal force. All units understand"
Everyone confirmed their assignments and went to work.

****

Jake scanned the four foot by four foot tunnel with the flashlight as they stepped over old crates of broken whiskey bottles and musket balls. The dampness and must smell was overwhelming as they passed through large cobwebs. Palmetto bugs the size of an index fingers were scattering everywhere as he moved the light from side to side. Lisa was holding onto his belt loop for her life, gasping at the site of spiders and bugs. Small puddles from the previous rains made breeding grounds for mosquitoes that were eating them alive. They had been hunched over for what seemed to be a mile, when Lisa tapped him on the back and asked him to stop and take a break. He stopped for her and turned around shining the light in her face. She was dirty with her black curly hair matted to her glistening face and cobwebs in her hair. He wiped the hair from her face and flicked a palmetto bug from her shoulder.

"I can't take this Jake; you know how much I hate bugs' she said as she wiped her face of mosquitoes.

"I know baby we got to keep moving, there's rats in here, mosquitoes probably feeding on 'me" he said.

"What does that mean" she asked?

"Malaria Baby. This tunnel hasn't had air in it for who knows how many years" he said.

"Where does it lead" she asked.

"I think it leads to Truman's Little White House, if I remember correctly" he said.

"Ok, while were walking can you please explain to me what is going on. People have died and the people who are after us are going to kill us" she said as she started to get choked up.

He grabbed her by the face and reassured her that nothing was going to happen to either of them and kissed her on the lips. She hugged him for a minute and trembled but all he could think about was what is on the the flash drive and why do these people want them so bad? What the hell was Jonathan into and why did he drag him into it? Not such a perfect Key West morning after all he thought.

He explained the whole morning to her. Every detail about the couple that was at his bar the night before. His usual morning walk to the coffee shop. About how he saw the same guy at Schooner Wharf and the little girl giving him the envelope and how he thought it was strange but didn't think anything of it. He told her that Jonathan was a hacker who stole movies and that he was dead and really had no answers to her questions. He wanted to know who these people were also and why they wanted the flash drive but he was as much in the dark as she was. He did know for a fact that if he didn't get her to safety and away from these people, they would both be dead.

"What are you going to do" she asked?

"Let's keep moving. We'll come out at The Little White House, but I promise, before we get there I'll have a little better plan. Steve's condo is around the corner. When you get there, stay with him until dark. I'll be able to make it to Ed's better alone" he said.

"They have tours in the daytime and people will be everywhere" she said.

"That's better for us. They won't hurt us in public. I think" he said sighing.

****

Commander Sinclair and Sgt. Taylor were looking over several blueprints of the fort on the laptop when a B212 helicopter came overhead and landed in the courtyard next to the Hummer. Four heavily armed men jumped out and ran over to the vehicle as the chopper lifted off and banked left toward the old Navy base. Sgt. Taylor got out of the Hummer and went to talk to the men, directing two of them to head to the south side of the fort and check the beach area.

"Taylor come here" Sinclair said.

The Sergeant hurried over to the Hummer and peered into the passenger window. On the tablet were two sets of blueprints side by side on the screen. They both were analyzing them closely when Taylor noticed something.

"Right there. Do you see that Sir" Taylor pointed at the screen.

"Looks like an error in the drawing on the West entrance over there" Sinclair said as he pointed at the blueprint.

"A tunnel within the tunnel Sir, but it doesn't show where it leads" Taylor said.

"That's their only way out. You and the Corporal find a way to get in there and get that flash drive Sergeant, and don't hurt them, understood" Sinclair said.

"Yes Sir. Corporal comes with me. Were going fox hunting" Taylor said to him.

They took off running towards the West cannon tower and disappeared inside. Sinclair looked in amazement at the two schematics and chuckled for a second and wondered how this kid knew about it. His E-mail flashed on the bottom of the screen, but before he could look at it a Key West Police cruiser pulled in behind his Hummer. The Officer got out and approached as Sinclair was exiting the Hummer to greet the officer.

"Commander Sinclair, officer. How can I help you" he said as he put out his hand.

"Barnett, Key West PD, How are you today" He asked shaking hands.

"Pretty good, Officer Barnett. What brings you to the fort?" Sinclair asked.

"Commander I was over on Simonton Street helping with crowd control for a possible murder or suicide. The Chief asked me come over and see why there was helicopter activity at the fort when there were no military exercises posted for this morning, sir" Barnett said.

"Murder over on Simonton, where" Sinclair asked.

"At the beach, Sir. It's undetermined yet but it will be an on-going investigation. Key West doesn't get too many murders and we treat every suicide like one" Barnett said.

"I understand and I apologize for this unannounced training drill, but my men needed a quick real time scenario to go ahead further with their objective. We'll need ten more minutes and be clear and tell the Chief thanks for his understanding" Sinclair said as he turned and walked back to the Hummer.

"No problem Sir. I'll tell him but next time clear it with the proper channels, OK" Barnett said.

Sinclair put his hand up in confirmation and walked back to the Hummer as Officer Barnett got into his cruiser and drove away. He ran his hands through his hair and leaned on the door and looked out towards the beach. He thought to himself that this situation was only slightly out of control, but what mission ever is in control. He reached into the Hummer and grabbed the head-set.

"Helo-one, do you copy" Sinclair said into his head set.

"Go to Helo-one" The ear piece rattled.

"Helo one-echo, Commander Sinclair here, take the bird back to base and standby, we're drawing some unwanted sightseers... Copy" Sinclair said.

"Copy Commander, flying Gulf side and heading back to the S.O.C" The pilot said.

Sitting in the Hummer Sinclair took a moment to think about the situation they were in. The KWPD was investigating the suicide as a murder and that meant the whole force would be working the case. The Chief will definitely call in experts from the mainland. Miami detectives were thorough but he had faith in his team. Taylor was good at his job and killing was his specialty. The investigation would conclude that it was a suicide and blow into the ocean breeze just like all the others that he had been involved with. He was sure of it.

"Commander" The radio chattered in his ear.

"Taylor go ahead. Give me something good" Sinclair said.

"We got it Sir. We got the tunnel and we're going in. The Brick is thick we might lose radio contact, Copy" Taylor said.

"Get in there Sergeant and bring me that flash drive, Copy" Sinclair said.

"Yes Sir, I'll confirm when we have subjects and the drive Sir" Taylor said.

Sinclair took the Radio and put it on the dash of the Hummer, leaned back and breathed a sigh of relief. Soon this whole mission would be over he thought. It had been thirty seven months that he and his men had been tracking Jonathan Pressley across twenty plus states and three countries. His hacker career was over, and for him Simonton Beach was the end. He looked over at the laptop and realized the inbox was blinking on his E-mail and scrolled the cursor over it and opened the inbox and hovered over the attachment. He clicked on it, looked at it in disbelief. The kid was a god damn Army Ranger and had been a sniper in Desert Storm, serving two years in Kosovo and had a purple heart. He snatched the radio off the dash and yelled for Taylor, but all he got was static and garbled voice in return. He jumped out of the Hummer and ran towards the north entrance calling for him to abort and return, but all he got was static.

****

They had been hunched over and crawling through spider webs for what seemed to be an hour when they came to the end of the tunnel. Jake shined the light on the brick wall and tried to figure out where the exit was when Lisa pointed to a lock on what looked like a wooden trap door above them. Just like everything at the fort the lock was over a hundred years old and needed a skeleton key to open it.

Jake put the back pack down and gave the flashlight to Lisa to shine on it. He tried pulling it from the iron loop of the lock with no avail. He reached in the back pack and pulled the handgun out and hit the lock with the handle trying to break it off when he saw a flash of light about sixty yards down the tunnel. He looked at Lisa then looked back down the tunnel. She must've noticed his expression and turned around to see what he was looking at. She turned around and pieces of lock came showering down on her as it broke off. He put the weapon back in the back pack and zipped it shut.

"Hurry. Push it open and let's get the hell out of here" she said.

"On three babies" he said.

They had to work fast. Jake stood up and with all his strength he pushed the trap door open. Glass crashed and furniture fell over as he climbed up into the dining room of the Truman's Little White House. He pulled her up onto the floor and as Jake closed the door he could see the flashlight getting closer. He acted fast and pulled a wooden cabinet over on top of the door blocking the men from getting in.

Lisa stood up and moved away just in time to not get covered by the falling trinkets and souvenirs. She could hear the men yelling through the floor as the door jumped up from them pushing on it. She moved away quickly from the door and flinched when Jake grabbed her by the arm and pulled her out of the way.

"Let's move. It's only a matter of time until they get through" he said.

"I'm Trying" Lisa said.

As they turned around to head for the front door they ran into a wall of tourists on a tour of the museum staring at them in awe. The tour guide walked over and looked at them, then leaned around to look at the trap door.

"I've been working here for thirty years and had no idea that was there" he said.

"I guess you learn something everyday" Jake said as they walked through the crowd and ran out the back door across the lawn.

They cut to the right and headed for the back gate when Jake looked back and saw screaming and yelling tourists fleeing the Little White House. He opened the gate and they ran down the alley between two buildings and headed for the Hyatt Hotel but darted into the two stories Hilton hotel parking garage, stopped and waited.

"We got to split up. You're two minutes from Stevie's house" Jake said.

"Why, I don't want to leave you alone. I don't want anything to happen to you" She said tearing up.

"I got to get over to see Ed and if you're not with me, you can't get hurt if they catch me" he said

She shook her head that she understood as he instructed her to head towards the lobby of the hotel, walk quickly through the front door and go straight for the pool. Behind the pool-bar was an exit that led to the Truman Annex and she would see Stevie's condo down the walkway on the left. He instructed her to go around the front of the condo in the lobby and take the elevator to his place and he would contact her in a few hours.

"What if he isn't there" she asked.

"He'll be there trust me. He drinks all night and sleeps all day and besides the key is under the door mat" he said.

She kissed him then turned and ran for the entrance of the hotel and vanished into the lobby. Jake darted across the parking garage and took the stairwell to the top deck and peered over the edge towards the Little White House.

11:50AM

Taylor could see the couple thirty yards away. He wanted to just shoot them to get the mission over with and go home, but the Commanders words rang in his head that there was to be no violence. He reminded the Corporal to shoot only if they fire first but just wound them. He looked at Taylor in disgust and kept on moving. He could see the girl was holding a flashlight and the man was hitting something when the tunnel flooded with light. They were within ten feet and they had them but before he could grab them, they climbed up into a trap door and the girl stood up in the opening. He was almost within reach of her when she was pulled up and the wood door slammed closed in the Corporal's face.

"God dammit" The Corporal said as he tried to open the door with his shoulder.

"We're not going to hurt you two, all we want is the flash-drive and you could be on your way" Taylor screamed through the floor hoping that they would just open it back up.

He waited a second to see if he got a response from the couple, but only the sound of footsteps running away from the trap door. He still didn't know where he was and his radio hadn't worked since they entered the tunnel. He tried it again but all he got was static.

"Move back NOW" He said as he unloaded the whole clip of the MP5S machine gun into the trap door.

Splinters dust and debris flew everywhere as the clip ran out, and Taylor motioned to the Corporal to finish the job on the door. He obliged and when he was done they were able to bust through the shredded wood and climb up after the couple.

Screaming people were running in every direction as the men reloaded their weapons and ran after them. They stopped and surveyed the area but, there was nothing only tourists in Hawaiian shirts running everywhere and no site of the couple.

"Commander, do you have a copy" Taylor said as he spoke into the head-set.

"Sergeant, have you retrieved the flash-drive" he asked?

"No Sir, they got away. They blocked the exit in the tunnel" Taylor replied.

"What is your location Sergeant" The Commander asked.

"We're at the Truman Little White House, sir. We made some commotion sir and the cops should be arriving any minute. We need an extract" he said.

"Of course you did Taylor. Get the hell out of there. I got some Intel you might be interested in. Head for Pier B, the boat will pick you up and don't upset the tourists. COPY that" he instructed.

Taylor and the Corporal were less than three hundred yards from Pier B trying not to make a scene as well as not getting ambushed. They jogged towards the pier as tourists stared and moved cautiously away from them. They were here somewhere in the crowd of people but he had little time for that now as the sirens from the Key West PD were blaring up Front Street towards their direction. It was time to get serious with this individual he thought, as they got to the end of the pier, their extraction boat pulled up.

****

Jake looked over the edge of the parking deck and could see the soldiers running past the Hyatt Hotel. His heart dropped to the floor. He thought they spotted Lisa running into the front entrance and sprinted around to the west corner and could see them moving past the hotel towards the end of the pier. She was in the clear. He took a deep breath and leaned against the wall regaining his composure, but there was little time for a break as the whole police department could be heard coming towards his direction.

He thought about going straight to the Key West Police. Whoever these guys were, they were not working with the local police and that was why the two men were heading for the pier. They didn't want to have ant confrontation with the authorities. He reached in the back pack and grabbed the cell phone and flipped it open to Steve's home phone number. Hopefully, Lisa had made it there. He wanted to call and tell her that he would be heading to the police to explain everything to them and for her to meet him there in an hour.

All of a sudden as he was looking for the number the phone rang in his hand, startling him. He looked at the caller ID and didn't recognize the number as it rang three more times and was hesitant to answer it. He thought it might be Lisa on another phone letting him know that she was ok; reluctantly, he answered it.

"Hello Mr. Jones, are we having fun yet" The voice said.

"Who is this" Jake asked?

"Never mind who I am, all I want is the flash-drive and we can call it even" The man said.

"Even from what? You sent two men to my house to try to kill me and my girl" he replied.

There was a little moment of silence on the phone and Jake was willing to work with the man to get out of this predicament. He had the upper hand, since he had the flash-drive and soon the local police would be on his side in less than ten minutes.

"Yes, I wanted to apologize for that but these are the kind of people that we are both dealing with. They truly have no value for life and they will stop at nothing until it's all over. You do remember those days when you were an Army Ranger, Sergeant Jake Andrew Jones" He asked?

"How could I forget those days? You sound like a Lieutenant or a higher ranking officer. It was people like you that made me puke my guts out that the taxpayers pay your huge salary's to make killing machines" Jake replied.

"You're a smart man Mr. Jones. Now be a smart man and give me the flash-drive before you or a loved one gets hurt" He said.

"See that's the shit that I never liked about the military" Jake said.

"What's that, son" he asked.

"Listening to jackasses like yourself for four years. Obviously you think you know everything since you're in command. But you've forgotten how long I've lived here" Jake said.

"I know everything about you Mr. Jones, including the fact that you're on the top of the Hilton Hotel parking garage as we speak" He said.

He looked at the phone for a second and knew he was in trouble. He stood up and looked around in all directions but there was nobody in the sea of cars. He took the 9mm out of the bag tucked it in the back of his shorts and put the flash-drive in his pocket and pitched the backpack in the trash as he walked towards the cars. He needed a change of clothes he thought as he walked towards the north exit.

"Yeah, I bet you didn't know this. I'm taking your flash-drive to the police and I'm going to tell them Jonathan was murdered for them. Then what are you going to do. Obviously you aren't working with them" Jake said.

"I wouldn't do that Mr. Jones. Since we've been speaking, you've just become a fugitive in South Florida. You're all over the news" he said.

He found a door open on a BMW that had some shirts in the back seat. He climbed in and snatched them as well as the sunglasses and Panama hat and put them on in the stairwell. He could see through the glass in the stairwell that there were several police cars on the street below.

"You tried to kill me, you piece of shit. I'll be coming for you" Jake said as he flipped the phone shut, walked down the steps and out into the crowd.

****

Sinclair looked at the phone for a second in disbelief. He speed dialed the S.O.C, the point of operations and connected with Maggie "the magician". He instructed her that the subject was uncooperative and they had to implement protocol seventy-nine. If anyone had the ability to get a subject flushed out it was her and soon Jones would be wanted by every law enforcement agency in the country.

****

Front Street was heavily crowded with passengers from a cruise ship that had docked earlier in the day. Jake walked past the front entrance of the Hilton Hotel and blended in with the tourist and headed down the street towards Fitzpatrick Lane and turned right. He took the cell phone out of his pocket, pulled the sum-card out of it and threw it into a homeless mans shopping cart full of clothes and junk. He turned left onto Green Street and ducked into Captain Tony's Saloon and waited to see if he had been followed. He blended in and hid behind some tourist by the front entrance so he could see down the lane he had just come from.

On the corner he could see a man wearing sunglasses and a Columbia fishing shirt talking to himself. The man looked irritated and was throwing his hand up when he turned and walked towards another man who was dragging the bum towards him by the collar. He handed the cell phone to the other man and opened the case; he looked at it, and then smashed it on the ground. They sat the homeless man on the ground asked him a few questions then took off in opposite directions.

"Get your ass back to Command Center; we're drawing to much attention. We'll let the local authorities get him.

Get Unit 4 and 5 over to his house just in case he doubles back" The Commander instructed.

"Unit one to all other units, abort and head for the Command. Four and five, you heard the Commander" he said.

Sinclair slammed the door to the Hummer and pounded his hands on the steering wheel. It should not have come to this and he didn't want to shed anymore blood but, orders were orders. He broke them once today and now the authorities will have every man in South Florida looking for him, which meant the flash-drive could be compromised. He had to put more pressure on him and it was time to get J.A.I.D. involved.

The Joint Agency on Internet Data was the watch dog of technology. It is governed by the appointed Internet Czar and controlled by the Joint Chiefs of Staff. The highly secretive facility monitors all internet traffic online for national security purposes. Every web site, every blog, every search and every transaction that is handled through the internet is being watched or monitored. They've been responsible for the capture of many fugitives, countless terrorist cells and low level criminals.

J.A.I.D. has facilities in several cities in the United States as well as a central location in Washington, D.C. NAS Key West, being the Southernmost facility has the highest amount of watchdogs with six thousand people logged into computers monitoring internet traffic from Georgia to Florida, all of the Caribbean, including the most important country, Cuba, and forty percent of South America down to Venezuela.

Commander Johnson, head intelligence officer at J.A.I.D. NAS Key West, and Commander Sinclair were Annapolis graduates and served together in Desert Storm and had been friends for twenty-two years. He always left the front door to his facility open for Sinclair's unit to obtain information on suspects. It was time to pay his old friend a visit, he thought as he started the Hummer, but first he had to go back to the S.O.C.

1:30PM

A half hour went by as he sat on the toilet thinking about what he was going to do. He needed to find a phone quickly, he thought, as he opened the stall and went to the sink and splashed some water on his face. He wiped his face with the paper towel and put the hat and sunglasses back on, walked back into the bar and stood by two girls that were talking at the corner of the bar. The girl to his left had her back to him and her purse was on her right. It was open and he could see her cell phone sitting in plain sight. He tapped the girl to his left on the shoulder and pointed across the bar and told her that Captain Tony was standing on the other side of the bar. The two girls stood up on their stools trying to get a peek of Tony when Jake snagged the phone from her purse and headed for the front door. He smiled for a second at the fact that Captain Tony had been dead for over a year, walked out onto Green Street and headed towards Duval Street.

He pulled the Sim card out of the phone and put his in its place and turned it on. There was no way they would be able to track him by GPS or monitor his calls now. He searched through his contacts to see who he could call to pick him up, but the only person nearby was Pat Conley from Billie's bar a block away. He dialed the number and Pat the bartender answered.

"Jake, my man, what's up" Pat said.

"I'm in trouble and I need your help" he said.

"What do you need" Pat asked.

"I need to borrow your car and use your office. Can you help me with that" Jake asked?

"No problem my friend, I'll see you in a few" Pat said as he hung up.

Key West was a close knit community. Once you lived there for several years friends became like family. They were the only ones you could depend on since most locals very rarely could get to the main land for a visit home. Everyone got along with each other because god only knew when some natural disaster would wipe out this little island.

He was a wanted man now, and there would be few, if none of his friends that would turn him in, because in the local's eyes it was the ultimate betrayal of trust. Nobody liked a rat, especially in the Key's.

He turned left and walked down Duval Street. It was crowded with hundreds of people from cruise ships. He looked down the street towards Hoggs Breath Saloon it was a sea of people entering and exiting retail shops and bars. He was a block away and it was perfect cover. He could've walked back to Fitzpatrick Lane and ended up in front of Billie's but didn't want to risk it since he had no idea which direction the other man went.

He weaved in and out of people, looking at every face, hoping that the two men didn't double back and trap him at Front and Duval. He cut through the parking lot of the Hogs Breath Saloon and ended up directly across the street from Billie's Bar. He walked through the crowd and stopped to take a closer look, hiding behind a large Banyan tree to see if it was all clear, then sprinted across Front Street into the bar. He went directly to the rear looking around to see if he had been spotted, but the only patrons were some locals sitting at the other end drinking and having a good time. For the first time today Jake knew he was safe.

"What can I get you Sir" Pat the bartender asked as he threw a drink coaster on the bar.

"It's me Pat" Jake said.

"Wholly shit dude, you look like a freaking tourist" He said laughing.

"How the hell do you think I got over here" Jake said.

"Word on the street is you killed Jonathan? And when was that supposed to have happened. You guys were friends" Pat said

"I'm in really deep shit. Can we talk in your office" Jake asked?

Pat walked over to the phone and called another bartender to come relieve him. They walked through the back and upstairs to the office where Jake collapsed on the couch in Pats office. He reached in the back of his shorts and pulled out the silenced 9mm and set it on the stand next to the sofa. Pat sat down at his desk and asked him if he wanted a drink and Jake nodded. He picked the phone up and called downstairs and two minutes later a waiter from the restaurant knocked on the door with a six pack of Heineken and Pat instructed the employee to leave it by the door.

"Nice gun, where you get it from" Pat asked.

"From the guy that tried to kill Lisa and me this morning" Jake said.

Jake sat back and Pat retrieved the six packs from the hallway and handed him one. He proceeded to tell him the entire events that took place this morning and explained to him that he didn't fire bomb the church in Miami and that he has been pursued relentlessly for the past several hours because of a flash-drive he had in his pocket. He showed it to Pat and explained the bizarre way Jonathan had given it to him.

They had been friends for years, but he looked at Jake in disbelief and asked to take a look at the flash-drive. He looked at it and was amazed at the amount of data that they could hold. Pat pointed out that it was capable of holding ten terabytes +and was curious to see what was on it.

"We can't do that" Jake told him.

"Why not? These people are trying to kill you. At least see what's on it" Pat said.

Jake explained to him that Jonathan was dead because of the flash-drive and that he knew the right person who could take a look at it and lead him in the right direction to clear his name. If anyone else knew what was on them, then they would sure as hell be dead also.

"I understand Jake but you know, and I know, and the whole Island knows that you're innocent. Whatever you need, I'm here to help" Pat said.

"I need your car and some cash. Can you help me with that" Jake asked?

"Of course Bro. I own this joint, remember" Pat said as he threw him the keys to his car and fished out a grand from the safe.

Jake was looking at the television behind Pat and grabbed the remote and turned the volume up. It was the afternoon news from Miami and his photo was on the screen. The news person was in front of a smoking church in Marathon, Florida, fifty miles from Key West and was reporting that eyewitnesses identified a man named Jake Jones as being responsible for firebombing the Church.

"Their setting me up, those bastards" Jake said as he slammed his hand down on Pats desk.

"No one is going to turn you in, relax" Pat said.

He suggested that Jake lay low for a few hours, take a shower and change into some of the extra clothes he had in the closet and leave when the sun went down. Wherever he was going he would be able to get there better in the cover of night.

****

The kid was on the run now, Sinclair thought. The amount of time that he had lived in Key West and the amount of people that he knew was making it more difficult to find him. He had many assignments on other islands and it was the same on this island as it was in the Caymans or anywhere else. There would be very little help from the locals.

He stopped the Hummer at the Navy entrance and showed the Private his credentials and entered the base. They drove around to the north side and parked in front of the S.O.C, where Taylor and the team had been waiting. He had been furious for the ten minute drive and this was the closest he had ever been to this particular threat. The operation had not been a success and the information had not been retrieved and he knew he would be receiving a call from his superiors soon.

Sinclair walked into the S.O.C and the team got into formation and saluted him. He instructed them to sit down as he walked to the front of the room. The facility resembled a call center with computers and monitors spread out in a large circle and in the center were multiple flat screen televisions on each side of a cube. The S.O.C was a staging ground for major missions in South America but currently there wasn't much activity to have it fully operational.

Sinclair was standing in front of a T.V monitor looking at the afternoon news from Channel 4 in Miami and what he was looking at amazed him. It was a photo of Jake Jones, wanted by the authorities for firebombing a church in the Marathon area. He turned and screamed at the team.

"Maggie, what the hell is this" He asked.

"What do you mean, Sir" she replied.

"You had him bomb a church, are you freaking nuts" He yelled at her.

You asked for protocol seventy-nine, and I did what you wanted. I got his name out there, correct" she said.

"Jesus Christ, you couldn't have made him a drug dealer or something. How many people did we kill in this process" he said.

"Absolutely none, Sir. The church was empty but the explosion was phenomenal. I had the team make it horrific to get the attention of the media and the ATF. It's amazing what resources we have at our disposal" she said.

Now the operation was truly botched. The cops and the feds are going to be all over Jones and it was inevitable the information had been compromised. The only way they were going to catch him now is if he tried to access the flash-drive, which will send and encrypted code to the S.O.C setting off in IP search of the computer that is being used, thus tracking the location of the user.

"Maybe this will work to our advantage. He's going to want to know why we're after him and the flash-drive. With the heat on him from the Feds, I'll bet he'll access them within a few hours" Sinclair said.

"He'll access them" Maggie said as she smiled.

"You're not off the hook yet, smart girl. Get me all of the IP addresses on this whole island, even static IP's" The Commander ordered.

"Taylor do a search for all high level computer techs from here to Key Largo, the rest of you try to explain to me what the hell happened at Jones' residence. Did anyone even think of looking his BIO to see if this man had a military record before we stormed the place like idiots" He yelled at the other team members.

They all looked at each other in search for the right answer but none of them had anything reasonable to say to the Commander as he paced back and forth looking at them with crazy eyes. He walked over to Taylor and leaned on the desk in front of him.

"Did you think of that before you sent two Navy S.E.A.L.S in there to get ambushed? Anyone" Sinclair shouted.

"What's the plan Sir" Taylor asked.

"We're going to put the heat on him. We're going to J.A.I.D." Sinclair said.

"What's J.A.I.D.?" Maggie asked confused.

****

The November sky was upon the island as the sun was going down. It illuminated the high dark clouds with purple and orange colors creating a breath taking spectacle for the sunset watchers on Mallory Square. He had seen hundreds of sunsets and each one reminded him of snowflakes, not one was ever the same. He referred to it as the best minute in life that earth can give to its children as the sun disappeared into the ocean.

Three horn blows from the cruise ship meant that it was leaving port and the town would be less crowded he thought as he put a long sleeve shirt on. He didn't get much rest since he was concerned with getting together with Ed and seeing what was on the flash-drive. First he had to call Lisa and keep her updated as to what was happening since she would be extremely worried after seeing his picture on the afternoon and evening news.

He dialed Stevie's number and she picked up the phone. They talked for fifteen minutes and he reassured her that he was ok and instructed her not to pay any attention to the media reports. He instructed her to call her old roommate on Ramrod Key and have him pick her up and to stay with him for a while until this was all settled. She was sobbing and begging him to give himself up but he told her that he wasn't going to go to jail for something that he didn't do but she was confused and was having a hard time understanding why he wouldn't. He also told her his next move and that they needed to keep what he was telling her to them and that he loved her and would be in touch soon.

It was ripping his heart out to be away from her but he needed to get into the flash-drive and use whatever information that was on it for leverage and to clear his name. Finally, the sun was finally down, and it was time to get to the bottom of this.

5:50PM

Jake left a note on Pat desk thanking him for his hospitality and headed downstairs. He ducked out the side alley and down towards his friends car that was parked in Mallory Square parking lot with its convertible top down. He jumped in and put the top up, snapped it locked and drove out of the parking lot. He checked the mirrors to see if he was followed and thought for a few minutes to calculate which route would be best to take and decided to cut up Whitehead Street to Catherine Street and come in the back way on Watson Lane.

He pulled up to the stop sign at Front Street and made a right and stopped in front of Billie's and honked the horn. Pat came running out to tell him not to go that way since the KWPD had a road block at Eaton and Whitehead Streets and they were looking for him. He wished him luck and Jake cut the little sports car down Fitzpatrick, made a left on Green and sped down Elizabeth Street which took him through Solaris Hill by the old Cemetery to Watson Street where Ed's shop was located. He wanted to be inconspicuous and cut across Truman Avenue and parked behind the adult video store, where he would jump the fence and enter Ed's computer shop through the back door.

He parked the car in the rear lot of the porn shop next to Ed's business and waited a few seconds. It was dark and there were several cars in the lot. He didn't see anyone lurking around as he climbed up on the trash can and hopped the fence to the back patio behind Ed's shop, landing on boxes of old computer parts and falling into the debris face first. Scrambling to get to his feet, the back door to the shop flew open and it was Ed, standing there with a sawed off shotgun pointed in his face.

"You better have a good reason to be back here, Son" Ed said.

"Don't shoot. It's Jake Jones, Ed. I don't know if you remember me" he asked.

They had met several times before at his place of work whenever the computers would crash and as he was holding the shotgun in his face he hoped that he would remember him. He knew more of Ed through people on the island and the rumor was the man had worked for the CIA. He was the only computer geek that had a Level Four military clearance which meant he was allowed to work on any base in the world. Known around town as the man that could retrieve information from any computer. He had been known to work with the local authorities in many child pornography cases and Jake knew he was the only man on the island that could help him without turning him in.

"Yeah I remember you. You're a wanted man, Jones and what the hell are you doing here anyway. Stay right where you are I'm calling the cops" Ed said as he leaned back in the doorway and picked up the phone.

"Please don't, I have some information for you to look at. Jonathan Pressley gave it to me. It could explain a lot" Jake pleaded.

"You know that two-bit hacker, Huh?" Ed asked.

"He gave me a flash-drive and I need your help to see what's on it" he said.

"He committed suicide this morning, you know that?" He asked.

"It wasn't suicide, he was murdered" Jake said.

"I usually don't help people that blow up Churches and are wanted by the law, but I always wanted to know what that little shit Pressley was up to" Ed said as he invited him in and walked to a room in the middle of the shop that had several computers and monitors.

Jake refrained from telling him that there were military personnel involved and decided it would be best to tell him after those facts after he looked at the information. He pulled the flash-drive out of his pocket and handed them over. Ed looked at it for a second and handed it back and told him that this was no ordinary flash-drive and advised him to destroy it. Jake insisted that he take a closer look at it and began to tell him of the day's events and that his life was in grave danger. Ed was reluctant, but as he looked at the anguish in his face and knew the young man was being truthful. The people who were after him were going to make him disappear. He snatched it from Jakes hand and put it in the USB port.

"This is some really heavy shit, you know that son. No ordinary flash-drive. It has a ton of information on it" Ed asked.

"I appreciate your help, Sir" Jake said.

"Probably going to regret this, but what the hell, here it goes" He said smiling.

****

Sinclair and his team were settled in at J.A.I.D. and updated his friend Commander Johnson on the mission. The football field sized room of computers and monitors which was operating on a skeleton crew since it was getting close to the end of the year. He was informed of the high level threat that his subjects had posed to the integrity of the United States but it was in Johnsons best interest that he was kept him in the dark about the deeper aspect of how the information was obtained.

Sinclair felt that he was betraying his friends trust by giving him limited information, but knew that it was in his best interest he didn't know all the facts. They shook hands and Johnson told him his outfit was at his disposal and if he needed anything to give him a call at his home as he left the building.

"O.K what do we have" he said to the team as the door closed.

"We're up and running. This is some pretty neat stuff, Commander" Maggie said.

"This is why we're here. Tonight, the Human Integrity Tactical Squad, will derail another threat to the United States of America and its partners, and secure the information so life as we know it will remain stabilized" Sinclair said, as he settled in front of the monitors.

Taylor informed him that he acquired information on three leading computer specialist and had their locations on satellite. He pointed to the three monitors in front of him.

From left to right all three screens were tri-split with actual, thermal and GeoEye imagery, the military's most powerful satellite that gathers aerial and geospatial information through high-resolution imagery. The actual satellite images were showing a blurry picture on all three monitors. Taylor explained that the faint image was due to the cloud cover that had rolled in earlier from the Northwest, but the thermal and GeoEye imagery showed crisp pictures at all three subject's locations. The first subject was in Marathon, the second on Summerland Key and the third in Key West. All three subjects had level two or higher security clearance with the military.

"We also have Units four and five surveying the subs house a quarter mile away, along with the ATF and KWPD, right" Sinclair said.

"Yes sir, I also put two teams at the Marathon and Summerland locations as well" Taylor said.

"I don't know how long the church bombing thing will stick once the ATF is able to log onto satellite imagery, I can't block their access to it forever" Maggie said.

"That's why we create a mid level scenario. Look at that shit. Try to fend them off for another 24hrs" he said as he pointed to the television.

She was the only non-military person on the team and was recruited from MIT six months ago and was learning everyday about the Task Force protocols. What she learned today was all about the amount of time that could be bought for the team to acquire a subject and she failed by giving them only a few hours. She couldn't afford to have the ATF or the local PD acquiring the subject before the team could and if they did, it could mean the end of her career.

She stood up and walked over to the huge seventy inch monitor to the left of the teams staging ground, turned around and smiled at the team. Everyone looked at her in anticipation as she began to explain the program that she implemented to track the encrypted program through the IP addresses within seventy five miles. On the bottom of the screen were binary numbers with hundreds of rows perpendicular with percentages of data usage on the top of each set of numbers.

"Just tell us the quick version Maggie" Sinclair said.

"The quick version, Ok" she said.

She looked a little puzzled for a second as she tried to gather words that would fit their intellect, and then proceeded to explain her design. The program was able to analyze all the IP addresses of every computer that was online in real time. When the flash-drive is put into a computer an embedded encrypted program that was attached to the information when downloaded opens an IP exchange. Kind of like a hand shake. The identity program boosts the suspects address through the network at Bell South and the local cable company. The IP address is narrowed down by a percentage of transmission or TX and located through the binary numbers on the screen. Once the address has been identified it retrieves the Mac address of the subjects modem through their main system and brings up their billing account information and their location.

"There are thousands of IP addresses on that screen. How do we know which one it will be" Sinclair asked?

"Oh. It will light up in red. Pretty neat huh. It's a spoofing program just like malware" She said as she smiled.

"Ok people. All we can do is wait" He said as he walked over to Taylor and instructed him to have the chopper on stand-by and their fast boat stationed off the south side of Sunset Key.

It was a gamble that the subject would be at any of the locations. He had embedded himself in the local community and all he could do is hope the trap would work. They needed to get to him before the threat got to him and the threat was inevitable. If the information was made public, civil unrest would be imminent.

****

It seemed like it was taking forever for the mini flash-drive to load. Ed explained that there was a massive amount of information that was being read and could take several more minutes. Jake stepped back into the doorway of the room. It had been crammed with too much computer equipment to fit two people and Ed turned noticed he was uncomfortable and turned the monitor his way for him to see.

He thanked him for taking the time to help him with his situation and Ed told to him that the thought of Jonathan killing himself, was heart breaking. He had talked to him just a few days ago and seemed in a good mood and that they had even planned a fishing trip to the Marquesas for the end of the month. To him Ed told Jake, that didn't sound like someone who was going to take their own life.

"Is the front door locked" Jake asked?

"I think so, check it. We don't need any more guests tonight" he said as he laughed.

He walked down the hallway and out into the lobby but stopped in his tracks as Ed screamed in delight and called for him to come back and take a look at what he discovered. He turned around and as he walked back into the hallway, Jake asked him what he had found, but before Ed could give him an answer; the power went out in the shop. It was pitch black and they couldn't see a thing.

"Probably nothing should be back on in a second" Ed said.

"I hope so" Jake said anxiously.

The buildings backup power supply kicked on and the monitors illuminated the room enough so that he could make his way back down the hallway, but before he could get to the end, the bell hanging from the front door jingled as it opened.

"Are you expecting anyone" Jake asked.

"Not that..." Ed started to say.

He couldn't get the words out fast enough as the small disk like object slid on the floor down the hallway and stopped in front of the door way to the computer room and exploded, instantly blinding both of them and shattering several monitors and the window behind Ed. Jake reached for the gun in the back of his shorts but was grabbed from behind and restrained with zip ties and thrown to the floor.

"Get the flash-drive and the old man" A female voice with an accent said.

"Are you the police" Jake asked panicking?

"In thirty seconds you'll be dead. If you don't do as I say, when I say, I'll leave you in the middle of Truman Avenue. Do you want to live" She asked?

"Yes. Yes of course" He said as he took a deep breath.

"Ok get them to the van we got 20 seconds. Blow the building" She yelled.

His vision was starting to come back as he and Ed were ushered out the front door and thrown into an awaiting van. Ed was on top of him and rolled over onto his back revealing the left side of the females face. She was dressed in commando gear, talking into a head set in English and giving the driver instructions on where to go in another language that Jake thought was Russian.

Ed sat up and leaned against the side of the cargo van and looked at Jake in disgust but couldn't say anything that was going to make his situation better. He wasn't forced by the young man, as if it he put a gun to his head and demanded that he looks at the flash-drive he thought. It was his own stupidity.

"What did you mean blow the building" Ed asked the woman?

The girl leaned over and looked through the back window of the van, looked at Ed and pressed the button on what looked like a remote detonator. The explosion was intense and the massive fireball plumed way up in the air as Jake and Ed turned around and looked out the back window. The night had been turned into day as the computer shop became nothing but dust and debris. Ed sunk his head in his chest as he witnessed the demise of his business.

"Sorry Ed. I didn't mean to get you involved" Jake said remorsefully.

"I should have been prepared for that. I'm getting rusty in my old age, I guess" He said as he managed to smile.

5:51PM

****

"We got him. He's accessing now" Maggie screamed with joy.

"What's his location, pin him down" Sinclair shouted.

She was typing as fast as she could to get the location of the IP, Mac and billing address as the series of numbers lit up on the huge monitor. Taylor was looking closely at the thermal image on all three monitors then looking over at her, waiting to dispatch his units and end this once and for all.

"924 Truman Avenue" She turned and said to Taylor.

"Units four and five, he's at 924 Truman. Proceed with caution" Taylor ordered.

"Copy that Sergeant" The units responded.

"We got him now. Get the chopper in route" Sinclair said as he paced back and forth looking at the monitors.

They were three blocks from the address and would arrive on site in twenty seconds as they turned the SUV around and made the left onto Truman. Not wanting to make any mistakes they loaded and checked their automatic weapons as they got within a hundred yards of the address.

Taylor was looking at the monitors and loaded a wider angle of a two block radius. He could see his guys speeding down Truman and focused on the address. There was a vehicle out front and the thermal image showed that it was running from the heat coming out the exhaust. Four people exited the building, jumped into the vehicle and began to drive north on Truman. He could see that units four and five were pulling up to the address at a high rate of speed then skidded in front of the building and stopped.

"All units get the hell out of there. Abort" he yelled into the radio. He could see on the thermal screen the units had exited the vehicle, and then tried to return to the SUV but the screen turned white from a massive explosion and ball of heat. He leaned back in his chair. The image was clearer as he could see the SUV had been blown onto its roof, engulfed in flames and his men lying on the ground.

"What the hell just happened" Sinclair screamed?

"Helo One" Taylor said.

"Helo one goes ahead" The pilot said.

"Our subject is in a van speeding north towards White Street, intercept. Units four and five are down" Taylor said.

"I don't give a shit what you have to do. Kill everyone in that van. If that flash-drive gets off this island, it's over. You hear me" he screamed into the headset.

"They got to him before we did. How did they do that" Maggie asked.

"Helo one your vehicle is a red van. It is turning right onto White Street. The use of deadly force has been authorized" Taylor commanded.

"Roger that. I got the vehicle in sight. Getting a lock and ready to engage" The pilot said.

****

They came to the intersection of Truman and White Streets, slowed down and made a right turn towards the Atlantic Ocean. Jake whispered to Ed if he had any idea who these two women were and Ed told them that they were probably mercenaries from another country. He thought they were either German or Polish, but couldn't make much sense of why they were still alive.

The blonde woman who had blown Ed's building up climbed into the back of the van and pulled a large knife from a sheath on her thigh and Jake scrambled towards the back of the van trying to get away from her but was stopped by a large case that blocked the two back doors. She stood over Ed, reached down and grabbed his hands and cut the zip ties from his wrists.

"The flash-drive, give it to me" she said as she stood over Jake.

Jake put his hands out and the women cut him loose then he reached in his pocket and gave her what she wanted. The last thing he needed was another confrontation, especially with this woman, he thought.

"We don't want to hurt you but if we have to we will. Your life and everyone's life is in danger" she said.

"Hey whatever you want from me, I'm good with it after the day I've had" He said as rubbed his wrists.

"Cholera mamy towarzystwo" The driver of the van shouted in some language...

"Co jest grane" she asked her.

"Helikopter" she said.

"What's going on" Jake asked?

"We got company, a chopper. Get to the front of the van" she instructed.

They both moved to the front of the van and Jake climbed into the passenger seat and looked into the passenger mirror and could see the helicopter coming in fast on them. The pilot was having a hard time getting directly behind them because of the large banyan and palm trees that lined the street. They crossed over Catherine Street and the driver floored the van swerving right, then left causing Ed and the other girl to fall to the floor of the van.

Jake looked in the side mirror and could see the machine gun flashing from the helicopter and the pavement being ripped up from the large bullets behind them. It was a matter of time before the van would be torn to shreds.

"Do something" Jake yelled at the girl.

They went under another large banyan tree at Washington Street narrowly plowing into a taxi as it sat at the light. It was torn to shreds as they passed and the car exploded as the bullets ripped through the car like butter. The chopper pilot was in trouble and pulled up as hard as he could barely miss the tree by inches. The girl in the back seized the moment and kicked open the large box by the rear doors, pulled out a rocket launcher and strapped it on.

"What are you doing" Ed asked?

"Going to take it down" she replied

"You can't fire that thing in here" He said.

"Just get down" she yelled.

They came out from under the tree canopy and floored it towards Seminole Street. From here there was no more cover. Jake looked out the window and could see the chopper had made a hard right and was circling back around.

"He's coming from the right" Jake said as he pointed out the window.

"I got him, just a little bit further she said as she kneeled down with the launcher on her shoulder.

"I'm asking you to please not to fire that weapon in this van" Ed yelled.

The chopper banked hard right and then made a left to come down and swoop in on them. Jake could see him coming in. He was about sixty yards out when he started to unload both machine guns. Bullets were ripping through parked cars and cutting through palm fronds as he dipped down and leveled off for a direct hit.

Jake watched her as she squeezed the trigger of the small rocket launcher and looked over at Ed who had his hands in his face. It produced no flame from the back of the launcher. The rocket shot three feet ahead of the girl then took off towards the helicopter. The pilot saw her as he leveled off and then tried quickly to climb out of the way, but it was too late as the rocket hit its mark and the chopper exploded, falling to the ground then skidding to rest in flames in the Botchi courts to the left.

"That rocket should have killed us" Ed said.

"It's a FIM-92. You can fire them indoors if you wish" She said as she closed the doors to the van and told the driver to head for the pier.

"That was a nice shot. What's your plan now" Jake asked?

"I got a Scarab waiting for us at the end of the pier. We'll get you on it and in a few hours you should have all the answers to your questions. My job was to get you and the flash-drive safely off the Island" she said politely.

"And what do we call you" Jake asked.

"My Name is Eva and that is Cloudia" she replied.

Minutes later they broke through the cement barriers at the entrance of the White Street Pier, drove to the end and parked the van where a black Scarab was waiting in the water for them. They exited the van and the two girls gathered their duffle bags from inside, threw them into the fast boat and climbed over the rail and jumped in. Eva told the driver of the boat to get moving as fast as they could, turn off the running lights and to head South East.

He did as she said and floored the boat and in a matter of seconds they were shooting across the Atlantic around 90mph. The wind was blowing hard which made the ride on the boat extremely uncomfortable and difficult for the driver to handle. Jake knew they had to move at these speeds, if not they would be caught or the hull of the Scarab would break and the boat would splinter into pieces. Whatever happens and wherever they were going, anywhere was better than being shot at.

****

Taylor and Sinclair looked at the infrared screens in horror as the rocket hit the chopper. The pilot's screams could be heard through their headsets as he went down in flames at the end of White Street and the van smashed through the barrier at the entrance of the pier. He zoomed in on the area and infrared picked up some heat coming from the water. He widened the area and zoomed in closer and could see it was some type of watercraft waiting for them.

No one anticipated this and his high speed assault craft was stationed off Sunset Key, almost five miles away. It would be a miracle if they were able to catch them.

"Assault craft one" Sinclair yelled into the radio.

"Assault craft one go head" the radio garbled.

"Helo one is down. Subjects are about to board some sort of watercraft at the end of White Street pier, intercept" Sinclair said.

"If we lose them, Sir" Taylor said.

"We're not going to lose them God Dammit" Sinclair said as he ran his hands through his hair.

They were all looking at the Commander as he paced back and forth feverishly looking at the monitors. They all knew that the ball had been dropped and knew they had not put forth the effort that they should have to obtain the flash-drive on this mission, but for most of the team it had been a long time working on this operation and they were extremely exhausted. If the boat got away there would be no way of knowing where the subjects would be heading and Taylor was praying that the assault boat would intercept.

Taylor uploaded some coordinates into the computer to have they Geo-Eye track the boat as it took off from the pier at a high rate of speed but the satellite was unable to load it to the specified area. It was moving out of the orbital parameter and the window was closing, and could see only a two mile radious and that was shrinking as well

Maggie tried franticly to connect to another satellite that was coming into their zone but they could see that the boat was too fast for them to keep up with it. Switching satellites would be useless after they loaded the coordinates. In twelve seconds they wouldn't even be on the same grid and their heading would be one of a million directions in which they could go.

"Radio, do you have better coordinates ASAP" the boat asked.

"Standby" Taylor said.

"They're getting away" Maggie said.

"No, they've already gotten away. We are all screwed do you know that? Does anyone know that?" Sinclair said as he looked at the monitors and picked up a chair and threw it through one.

"We tried Sir, and we underestimated them and a bartender from Key West who happened to be in the military, it's our entire fault Maggie said.

"No shit we did. First thing I want from all of you is to find out how they found him before we did. Second I want all Intel from everywhere. All Emails, cell phone calls, everything. If someone takes a shit and it smells like Intel, I want to know about it. Third, Taylor keep an eye on Jones' parents" he said screaming.

"You think he'll try to contact them, Sir" Taylor asked?

"I doubt it and Taylor, find that girlfriend of his also, it's a shot in the dark but he might contact anyone of them" Sinclair said.

"The threat already has him and the flash-drive. What good would all that does since they'll be able to fully exploit the information?" Maggie said.

"Maybe, if we find her we could use her to get Jones to give up their location" Taylor said.

"Also we're going to have Commander Johnson dispatch an Archangel A-12 recon aircraft in the morning to survey all vessels in a thousand mile radius. I'm heading to the

Pentagon to debrief the Joint Chiefs of Staff and to elevate the threat level to Red. But first I gotta go down to the crash site and smooth this shit over with the local authorities" Sinclair said as he kicked a chair out of the way as he walked out of the room.

6:20PM

The Scarab had already traveled eight miles and surprisingly they had not been followed. Jake looked behind them and he could see the lights of Key West but ahead it was pitch black as they came to the shelf of the reef. Ed yelled for the driver to slow down or they would bust the hull of the boat wide open as they passed Sand Key. The coral shelf ended and the ocean dropped off to a thousand feet and the waves would be much, much bigger.

As the forty foot boat slowed down Jake wondered if he was ever going to see Lisa or Key West again. He wanted to know where they were going but refrained from questions until they reached their destination. The girls had saved their lives and he didn't want to be rude but, Ed on the other hand, didn't have any manners and questioned why they had to blow up his shop.

"It gives us an advantage every time we can take out a member of the HITS squad" Eva said.

"What is HITS" Jake asked?

"The Human Integrity Tactical Squad. The world is not what you think it is, Mr. Jones" she said.

Cloudia, the other girl who hadn't spoken a word until now explained to them that they had to do everything necessary to obtain the flash-drive. She also told them that they would be introduced to the right person that had all the answers to their questions in a few hours, but Jake persisted.

"How did you know where to find the flash-drive" he asked?

"That's a good question" Ed said.

"Yes it is. First you have to realize something about the flash-drive" she said.

She began to explain to them how Jonathan had been working for several years on hacking into the Department of Defenses extremely top secret data bases along with a few other computer geniuses to elaborate on a theory. The information that he obtained came with a price. The DOD attached a super encrypted replicating program to the master files that he downloaded and copied, which set off the alarm at the HITS headquarters in the pentagon. Unknowingly, every time the information is uploaded to a computer, the program accesses the data base automatically. He had been pursued relentlessly by the DOD and HITS for over three years. But not until recently he was able to obtain all the information that would expose the governments for all the misery they have inflicted on their own populations and Jonathan paid the ultimate price for that information.

She continued to talk about how information was sent through a network, about capturing packets and breaking into nodes and how the information highway works. Jake was lost but Ed was like a little kid staring at his teacher in awe as she continued to delve into terms that Jake couldn't comprehend. He kindly interrupted and asked her to explain it a little slower and speak to him like he was technologically illiterate and to dummy it down for him.

Ed turned to Jake and explained the process of how they were able to intercept the information that the flash-drive was transmitting, capturing then decoding it and pinpointing where it was coming from. The process was super fast with millions of tiny bits of information being frozen then read, then thawed and sent on its way to its destination in micro seconds. In that small fraction of time they were able to read the IP address form the packet, thus linking it to the shop where the flash-drive was being uploaded into a computer.

"Neat stuff, Jake. I had read about that in some computer magazine. This just shows you digital information is not as safe as you think" Ed said.

"We have to stay one step ahead of them. We are constantly updating our equipment and finding new ways to obtain more information. Their process was similar to ours but ours was faster, we just beat them too you by sheer luck" Eva said.

"I know the government is shady, but what had Jonathan found that would cause a national crisis" Ed asked.

"It isn't government, its governments working together but once we get to our destination, Dr. Winslow will answer all of your questions" She said.

"Dr. Terrance Winslow" Jake said.

"That's correct" Eva replied

"Didn't he die three years ago in the Rocky Mountains" Ed asked?

A few hours had passed and Jake figured they were getting close to the coast of Cuba. Eventually they would have to rendezvous with another boat or the scarab will eventually run out of fuel. He was freezing and damp from the waves misting in the wind and hoped that the next stop or vessel they get on has a roof and a bar because after today's events he sure could use a drink. He was having some anxiety issues and was not amused by the situation he was in. He really had no care for their cause or what they were fighting for, but he had to respect them since they saved his life.

When he was in the military he had never been a fan of terrorism or government wars. He fought in Desert Storm and believed the war was motivated by a country that had an insatiable appetite for oil and was reluctant to go but took an oath to defend his country of all threats, foreign and domestic. Now, he was in a war which was no different from any other. It was the same rich person's war, sponsored by rich people, and making rich people richer, even if the Doctor had been declared dead, it was not Jakes war to suffer through.

Dr. Terrance Winslow was a self made billionaire who went missing on a solo flight from Las Vegas to Denver in the fall of 2006. He was presumed dead after an extensive search of the mountainous area where his aircraft was last reported. His body was never recovered and after the spring thaw, hikers found aircraft debris on a mountain slope believed to be Winslows but no human remains were ever found. Authorities believed that if the good doctor could've survived the crash, he would've never survived the harsh winter and extreme elements of Mother Nature. Eventually the search was called off and the story of the billion dollar man faded from people's memory.

Jake remembered reading the story in the local newspaper and followed it for several weeks until there was no more news of the man. Many people had speculated that the whole scenario had been staged and hearing that the Doc was alive and well, added new questions to the hundred that he had prepared an hour ago. He had seen many movies of billionaire madmen who wanted to take over the world and truly hoped that this was not the case with Dr. Winslow.

****

Sinclair turned left onto White Street and pulled the Hummer over in front of Sandee's Coffee Shop at the corner of Virginia Street. Through the windshield he could see from the carnage it was not a precision military effort by the chopper pilot. The Key West Fire Department was putting multiple car fires out along the street as people stood behind yellow police tape shooting video and taking pictures of bullet riddled vehicles. It was a disaster that was going to make headlines all over the world and Sinclair knew he had some explaining to do, and it wouldn't be the truth.

On his way down to the crash site he reluctantly decided on the terrorist angle for a cover up. If he told the media the truth, which he couldn't it would provoke more questions from them. In his mind the people responsible for this tragedy were terrorists and the American people were hell bent on squashing terrorism on their own soil. It made collateral damage look more appealing and the military look less trigger happy. His superiors wanted the public to view them as protectors, not as killers of young Americans hacking into government data bases and raising questions about the type of information that was stolen. Besides, to him, convincing some local police chief what happened was going to be easier than explaining to his superiors why they missed an opportunity to retrieve the data that threatened national security.

However the explosion on Truman Avenue would be harder to cover up. His team was virtually non-existant and the ATF and the local FBI would be more inquisitive of who his agents were. They would also be familiar with the owner of the computer shop since he had worked some cases for them and would certainly try to pressure him for his wherabouts. He decided to take care of the police chief first and let his damage control team work with the ATF and the FBI for a few minutes. By the time he made it to the site of the explosion they would be convinced it was a terrorist cell responsible for the bombing.

He pulled the Hummer to the intersection of White and Catherine Streets where a yellow cab sat smoldering. The officer who had approached him at the fort earlier in the day happened to be directing traffic but Sinclair couldn't remember his name when he pulled up to him. He rolled the window down so the policeman could see his face and the officer greeted him, Barnette his name plate said.

"Hello Commander, I'm going to guess that the helicopter down the street is yours" Barnette quipped.

"Barnette, one of these days you'll make a fine detective. Where's the Chief at son" Sinclair said trying to smooth the situation over.

"He's at the crash site. I'll radio that you're coming. Oh, and just to let you know, don't be surprised if he gets in your face, Commander." Barnette said with a smile.

Sinclair smiled at the smug little prick and drove around the smoldering cab. Most of the vehicles on the right side of the street were destroyed and the pavement was turned into

Swiss cheese from the twenty caliber rounds. Amazingly there were no fatalities he thought as looked down the street where the chopper had crashed, cutting a swath through palm trees and landing in the sand of the Botchi courts.

He climbed out of the Hummer and walked over to the chopper as they were pulling the charred remains of his pilot from the wreckage and took a deep breath as he surveyed the area. He noticed the Chief was moving fast in his direction but Sinclair didn't have time for the tirade that he was about to unleash on him. He wanted a little more time to grieve for his fallen soldier.

He had to rethink the whole situation and the events leading up to this young soldier dying today and this situation should've been under control earlier in the day. Now, he had to tell this soldier's wife that her husband would not be coming home to her and their small children.

Chief Randall Jennings was a short, chubby, hill jack transplant from the mountains of Tennessee. He was chosen over several other candidates because as a Leutenant for the Tyler, Tennessee Police Department, was solely responsible for breaking up the states largest methamphetamine lab which produced a street value of over twenty- million dollars worth of the drug a year. Some people say it was pure luck but the Key West Review Board responsible for his hire, believed he was capable of ending drug smuggling to the Island forever but in the three years leading the department his tenure has been plagued with corruption and scandals from the beginning.

"Chief Jennings, under military jurisdiction, I'll be limited on the information that I can give you, so let's make this quick" Sinclair said to him before he could speak.

"Commander, as mad as I am at this tragedy and the fact that it happened here in paradise, I trust your judgment on your operations here in the Keys, but why in the hell didn't you keep my Department informed of a security threat on my Island" the Chief said.

"Well, Chief when you have a situation that unfolds at the blink of an eye you have to do what you have to do. You of all people know what I'm talking about" he said passifying the man.

"Absolutely Commander, did you want to get the crime lab down here and investigate this or will the ATF and FBI taking over" the Chief asked.

"No the only crime is my dead pilot. My team will take care of this situation and have it cleaned in a few hours. Thank you Chief. Again, I do apologise" Sinclair said as he started to walk back to his vehicle.

"OK Commander. Oh, by the way does the name Jonathan Pressley ring a bell" he asked.

"Never heard of him, Chief. Why you ask?" Sinclair said as he looked towards the pier.

"We found him dead at the end of Simonton Street. Looked like a suicide this morning but now it's turned out to be murder. Some low life hacker, never heard of him, huh?" The Chief persisted.

"Hey Chief, I never heard of him or of a suicide this morning" Sinclair said as he walked over to his vehicle got in and drove to the end of the pier.

Sinclair saw in the Chiefs face that he knew he was lying since his kiss ass Officer informed him of their convesation this morning. He didn't care what the Chief thought as he drove past him and headed for the pier. He wasn't going to let the local authorities piece the day's events together and possibly create media frenzy. At all cost, no information would be leaked of a connection to Jones, Pressley and the day's events. All the media would know is that the two are connected and are a product of an unorganized terrorist cell that would be taken out in the next twenty-four hours. That was something he was sure of.

7:30PM

Jake could see pilothouse lights from a vessel seventy-five yards ahead, but couldn't make out the type in the darkness and estimated they had traveled at least eighty-five miles in four to six foot waves which dropped down to three foot waves. He wasn't much of a sailor but he knew they were close to land. Many times he had been in high seas but not at the speeds they had been traveling and his stomach was sick and queasy from the sloshing of the waters. His bones hurt and he was eager to get off the scarab get his land legs back.

Ed on the other hand was practically sleeping as they pulled closer to the stern of the pewter colored boat. Flood lights powered on and the rear of the boat illuminated allowing them to see the impressive looking one hundred fifty foot super yacht.

They tied the Scarab to the yacht and Jake noticed it had an intriguing name that he had never seen on a boat before and asked Ed what it meant. He told Jake he didn't know but thought the last word meant "white" in french as they climbed on the landing of the stern and went up the ladder onto the aft where an elderly man in a white jacket stood with terrycloth towels in his arms.

Eva stepped in front of them and immediately asked them each for thier cell phones as they climbed on board. They both looked at each other and without hesitation handed them over to her. She informed them that they would get them back in the morning and that it was only a precautionary measure. She explained to them that they would make the phones untraceable and Jake liked that idea and was beginning to feel more comfortable in seeing that they had what seemed to be a well put together plan.

They stood by the table and looked around in amazement at the five plasma televisions surrounding the oak bar with seating for twelve. There were Ports and Cognacs that Jake had never seen before which he imagined had to be pretty pricey, but what impressed him the most was that Dr. Winslow had draft beer on tap. He was beginning to like the guy more every minute, even though he was supposed to be dead.

The girls walked past and told them that they could help themselves to a cocktail or two and went through an automatic sliding door into the next room. He obliged and walked behind the bar, opened the cooler and pulled out an oversized mug and poured himself a draft beer. Ed asked him for a scotch on the rocks and Jake gave him some Johnny Blue over two cubes and slid it down the bar.

He took a long draw from the frosty mug and looked over at the man in the white jacket and Jake introduced himself and asked him if he would like anything. He said his name was Elliot, then thanked Jake but declined the offer and informed them that Dr. Winslow would be down momentarily.

Ed looked confused as he swallowed the last gulp of scotch and slid the glass towards Jake and gestured for a refill. He was jittery, looking at everything around him and grabbed the glass before Jake could finish filling it. Jake leaned into him and asked him to relax a bit, and reassured him that this was not the end of the line for either of them but Ed nervously slugged the whole glass anyway.

"Why do you think that is" Ed asked.

Don't really know. I should've been dead five times today. Besides why would they bring us all the way out here to kill us? They could've left us at the pier "he replied.

"They could've spared my shop. That was my life" he said shaking his head.

The sliding doors opened and Eva walked past them towards the Scarab. They stopped their conversation and attentively watched her. She had discarded her combat attire for a more casual outfit of shorts, sandals and a light sweater. Her long blonde hair blew in the wind as she leaned over the stern and gave the driver of the Scarab instructions as he started the boat, then sped south.

She was stunningly gorgeous Jake thought as she walked to the bar and sat down and asked him for a glass of wine. He poured her drink and the engines of the yacht came to life and began moving towards the southern Caribbean.

****

Sinclair walked to the back of the van at the end of the pier and looked inside. The ignition had been punched out and the vehicle was obviously stolen but what intrigued him most was the large military case that he was all too familiar with. He climbed in the back and opened it up and looked inside, when his phone rang.

"What did you find out Maggie" he asked as he shut the lid to the box and sat down.

"Well sir, they have advanced further than we anticipated" she said.

She explained to him how they were able to hi-jack into the main cable node several miles up the Keys and used a packet encapsulate to read every transmission and intercept the data before the imbedded program even registered to their computers. She had heard of the process of packet freezing at a data transmission conference at Harvard a few years earlier and that the process was far more advanced beyond the military's standard equipment. She knew of only one person capable of designing a program of that magnitude, and he had been reported missing a year ago.

"Really advanced stuff, Sir. Unfortunately they got the drop on us" she said.

"It takes money to be get this far advanced. Let Taylor know they used a FIM-92 to take down the chopper and have him meet me at the jet at 2200 hours, got it" Sinclair said.

"Where are you heading, Sir" she asked

"We're heading to Washington. I'm sending you the serial number of this rocket. Trace it to the money and find out who sold them this rocket. He could be our connection" he said.

He hung up the phone, snapped a photo of the rocket and sent it to Maggie so she could trace its route to the United States, if there was one. His phone rang again and it was the Department of Defense. He knew they would be calling but not this soon he thought as he looked at the phone. He answered it and spoke briefly informing his superior's that he would be landing at midnight for a debriefing. It would be a long night and he'd have to skip talking to the Feds at the site of the explosion on Truman Avenue. He had his own damage control to deal with back In D.C.

8:05PM

Dr. Winslow came through the sliding door and introduced himself to his guests and welcomed them to the new "White House" as they call it in French, La Maison Blanche. He was an eloquent man in his mid-sixties about five-ten with gray hair and in quite good physical shape for his age. Jake had read many articles about his adventures in some science and travel magazines, especially his five non-stop circumnavigations of the globe in a hot air balloon. His endurance of many hours in his last balloon flight around the world and numerous hiking expeditions to the top of Mount Kilimanjaro meant the man had to be in excellent physical condition.

Jake was beginning to think the man had totally gone nuts, just like in the movies, and that Winslow was another billionaire poised for world domination. He was going to take over the world from a super yacht that must have cost an easy fifty million and named it the White House. This seemed cliché and somewhat irritating that he wound up in a situation with a madman who had obviously lost all his marbles and dragged everyone in to his ridiculous plans. He was losing patience with him as the minutes ticked by and wanted to flee the yacht as soon as he had the chance. The boat had to be close to land and if he had to he would just jump over the side, say Adios to this lunacy and swim south.

Winslow walked past the bar area towards Elliot and exchanged words with him, then took a seat in one of the high leather chairs next to Eva. He sat there for a minute with his hands on his lap looking at Ed and Jake with a slight smile on his face. It made Jake feel uncomfortable so he asked him if he would like a drink and he pointed at the draft beer tap.

"It has been an extremely tumultuous day for the both of you, and I realize that you have a tremendous amount of questions for me, but first I would like to say some words of gratitude towards the both of you" He said as he got up and walked in front of the bar and stood before his guests.

He held his glass in the air and thanked the two men for the sacrifices that they had made earlier in the day and for keeping the flash-drive safe by risking their life and ultimately, letting the world know the truth. He praised Jonathan Pressley for being diligent in finding the resources for what will make the population open their eyes to the horrible lies that the leaders of the world have been letting them believe.

He informed them that the massive amount of information that was obtained from the governments would not have been able to be brought to light if it were not for the people who believed that there is a pandemic of injustice in the world and those individuals were the ones who made it possible for more people to see for themselves the travesty that is happening.

Dr. Winslow hadn't shed any light as to why they were on the yacht but whatever Jonathan was into, was obvious the Doctor had great admiration for him and Jake respected that, raised his glass as well and toasted to Jonathan, because he had been his friend.

"What is on the flash-drive that's so venerable to the government" Jake asked?

"That's a really good question. It's not what's on the flash drive; it's where it can take you and what it can show you. But we'll get to that soon" he said.

Jake assumed that it was going to take some time to get an explanation for the day's events so he poured himself another beer and waited for the man to continue. He was anxious for answers but was thankful to be alive and thankful to be aboard a fine yacht. However, there was only one place that he wanted to be right now and it was in the arms of his girl, Lisa.

The Doctor explained that it was not a coincidence that he and Jonathan had met while he and his wife were on a ski trip in Vale, Colorado in 2003. In fact Jonathan had searched him out. They became friends and even gave him a job at his Palo Alto, California research facility after he had personally checked out his references and found that the man was a brilliant programmer. By 2004 he had excelled at the facility and was spearheading a project that would help paraplegics walk again by using micro-processors to reconnect the spinal cord and transmit signals to the lower extremities. The project would give tremendous hope to people that would never walk again.

What impressed him the most, was the lack of education that he had acquired and never attended, or took a computer class in his life. Self taught from the time he was four years old was what Jonathan would tell the Doctor when they would go on trips together. But by 2005, unfortunately, the program was put on hold by the government and Jonathan became discouraged it was about to be shut down when they were so close to helping people walk again.

He went on to explain that in January, 2006, Jonathan flew to his vacation home in Miami to inform him that he was leaving the company and believed he had information that the Doctors life was not only in danger, but it would end soon. He thought Jonathan was crazy and possibly upset about the program ending and reassured him that he was a valuable asset to the R&D facility.

He persisted about having information of his demise then handed him an envelope, walked out the door and got in his car and drove away. Winslow said he don't open the envelope for several weeks and assumed that it was his resignation papers. Then one day in February after a golf outing at Miami Country Club he came home, sat at his desk, noticed the envelope and decided to open it. Inside on a note was an address and what looked like numbers to a combination lock in Stuart, about forty miles away. At the bottom of the note it stated that his life was in danger.

He became increasingly more paranoid about the letter and after several days of sleepless nights he decided to take a ride to Stuart and do a little more investigating. He was skeptical about the whole trip but couldn't stop thinking that there was a real possibility that his life was in danger. He had met many eccentric people in his days of making his fortune in the development of software and computer chips over the past thirty years, had his life threatened countless times, and hundreds of letters from psychotic people wishing death and destruction to his family and his empire. However, eccentricity was not a substantiated case for psychosis he thought as he packed an overnight bag that included a chrome plated forty-five, mapped out the directions and headed for the location that Jonathan wanted him to go.

He drove for an hour across the Everglades and picked up Interstate 75 north and entered the small town of Stuart, Florida. At the tip of town he stopped at a gas station and asked the attendant if he knew of a street he had written on a piece of paper. The young clerk instructed him to head out to the orange groves and take a left at Old Mill Rd. He looked at the Doc curiously and asked why he was going out to the old farm. It had been abandoned years ago, and all that was out there was the rubble of an old hay barn. Winslow smiled and thanked the clerk, walked out the door and looked down the street. It was early and the town was deserted.

He followed the instructions the clerk gave him and pulled up to the long driveway where a house once sat, stopped the SUV and retrieved the pistol from the bag. It was pitch black in the country and he was getting freaked out as he drove down the long driveway and stopped in front of the remains of an old barn and shut the vehicle off. He opened the glove compartment and took his flashlight out and walked towards the crumbled remnants of a barn with the firearm in his right hand.

The moon was bright and as his eyes adjusted he could see that the doors and part of the roof had fallen from the years of decay. He walked inside and clicked the flashlight on and panned it in all directions. He wished he had gotten more info from Jonathan as he walked through the cob webs towards the back where there was a large amount of old beer bottles and empty liquor boxes that had been discarded after some partying. It was late and there wasn't any partying going on tonight as he ducked under a few wagon wheels hanging from the rafters and came to an end. There seemed to be nothing in the barn except for dead pigeons and old beer bottles.

He had no idea what he was looking for as he shined the light up towards the ceiling and noticed something was written faintly in fluorescent spray paint on a rafter that kept the barn from falling down but could see only a little of the paint. He put the gun in the back of his pants and climbed up a ladder to the hayloft and shined the light on it but still could not read it so he shimmied out on to the beam and brushed the dirt from the paint. It was much clearer, "A capite ad calcem" it said.

"That's odd" he said out loud as he looked at the Latin phrase.

Fifty-five years ago he had been an altar boy, but that had been a long time ago and his Latin was minimal at most he thought, as he climbed back over to the hayloft and sat there looking at the saying. It had been the only saying among all the other graffiti written in Latin in the barn and he was struggling to remember what it meant so he pulled out his phone and decided to look it up online but he had no connection out in the country.

He climbed back down and stood under the beam and shined the light on the saying and like the light bulb turning on it was all clear. "From Head to Heel" it said as he looked down at his feet and kicked some dirt away revealing a large slab of cement. He found the edges of the slab and brushed the dirt away from the ten by six monoliths that had to weigh a ton and wondered how he was going to move it. He scraped some more dirt away from the edges revealing some heavy chains with hooks attached.

He turned the flashlight off and walked over to the entrance of the barn to see if he was still alone, propped the door open and looked down the road about a quarter mile from the barn as he walked to the SUV. It was all clear, no sign of headlights or anything as he turned around and backed up to the large slab and hooked the chains to his tow hitch, pulling the slab about ten feet. It was heavy enough it lifted the truck off its front wheels from its weight. He backed up and released the hooks from the truck and pulled the vehicle around the back of the barn out of sight, then went back inside and closed the door behind him.

He walked over to the hole where the slab had been and turned the light back on and peered in to see a long flight of cement steps that descended about twenty five feet down. He looked around again and took a deep breath and went into the hole. The dust was thick from the dirt that fell into the hole as he went down the thirty plus steps and came to a large wooden door locked with an old combination lock. He reached in his pocket and pulled out the note with numbers on it that Jonathan had given him and spun the dial to the lock. He couldn't believe it as the lock popped open. He removed it and pushed the door open and shined the light inside illuminating a long tunnel approximately thirty yards long. He went inside and closed the door behind him and fiddled for an inside lock and found it which made him feel better. Nothing could sneak up behind him now but was extra cautious about what was ahead.

It was very well constructed of smoothed poured concrete which had to take several years to complete he thought as he walked down the cob web filled corridor. There were no visible signs of people or footprints coming or going as he shined the late on the dust covered floor then turned left and descended another flight of steps taking him further into the ground. Once, at the bottom of another thirty steps he came to another wooden door but it didn't have a lock. He squeezed the handle of the door and pushed it open and shined the light inside and notice light bulbs hanging from the ceiling. He looked around on the wall by the door and found a switch, flicked it and the room illuminated. He was surprised there was power but also shocked at what he had discovered.

"Well what was it" Jake blurted out as he poured another beer from the tap.

"Let us finish this conversation over dinner, say we" The Doctor said as Elliot entered the aft and gave him a nod.

****

Sinclair pulled up to the Learjet on the southwest side of the Navy base where Taylor and Commander Johnson were awaiting. He knew the DOD and the Joint Chiefs would be calling in Johnson to have him assess the situation, since he was in charge of the lower 48 division of intelligence. He was a good man but Sinclair believed that he was going to have a hard time digesting the information that he was about to receive. His wife had died two years ago from an inoperable brain tumor and what he was about to hear was going to make him furious. Even if he knew what he was about to know now, wouldn't have made a difference since the international agreement stated that "under no circumstances" not one person was to be saved, regardless of their prominence or geniality in life.

Her funeral had been unsettling for Sinclair but he was a third generation enforcer of the code just like his father and his grandfather who piloted the program since its inception in 1943. He was dedicated and believed what HITS stood for and didn't let his emotions get in the way of keeping the code safe. Over his lifetime he held the secrets of many people he knew in the past and present but it was not his duty to break the code, no matter how close they were to him. It was that code that made this planet what it is today and if not for what he stood for, the impact on the planet would be devastating to the existing human race.

He unloaded his duffle bag and walked towards the jet and decided that he would slowly explain the situation to Commander Johnson over the three hour journey to the White House. He was not the only one who had to be informed of the threat; the newly elected President had to be informed as well. Guilt will fill Johnson because he couldn't save his wife but the new Democratic President elect will have a hard time understanding that his great country would be involved in such horrific atrocities. Sinclair knew it wwould not be received well by the President because the last four he had to inform did not go as well as he had hoped for.

They settled into the six- seated Jet and got ready for takeoff. Taylor sat in the back and Johnson by Sinclair buckled them in. It was going to be a long two hour flight and he needed to collect his thoughts, especially what he wanted to say to Commander Johnson. He had a big job ahead he thought, as the plane took off for Ronald Reagan International Airport. He had decided also that he would let the Secretary of State explain most, if not all of the details of the program to the President when they reached Washington.

****

9:00PM

The five of them entered through the sliding doors. They turned right towards the stern into a great room that was used for entertaining guests then turned left and walked down a long hall. They took an elevator to the upper deck where the main dining area had a view of the port side of the yacht. Everything sparkled and shined as they walked into the dining area where dinner was waiting at a large oak table that sat twenty people.

Ed and Jake looked at everything the boat had to offer, including a five thousand gallon fish tank built into the wall behind the dining table. There was hundreds of fish that had to cost thousands of dollars as well as the six plasma televisions that were mounted in various positions in the room. The decor was impeccable with fresh cut flowers placed on every coffee table that were in front of several leather couches. Jake noticed Dr.Winslow even had his own walk in humidor which had several thousand cigars waiting to be smoked. This to him what heaven was like he thought as he walked around the room and looked at some of the paintings hanging on the wall.

"Please have a seat gentlemen, dinner is getting cold" Elliot said as he pulled out a chair for Eva.

"Dr. Winslow. I don't want to be rude, but if you wouldn't mind me asking, what is the price tag on this boat" Jake asked?

"This yacht is one of a kind. Built by Phantom Yachts and has a price tag of around fifty million. I liked them so much, I bought the company" he said laughing.

"Speaking of money, Sir. If you're supposed to be dead, how did you get to keep your fortune" Ed chimed in.

"Offshore bank accounts. Cayman, Montenegro, places like that. I moved my wife to where we'll be traveling to tomorrow. But in the mean time let's eat and let me finish what I was telling you" he said as he took a sip of water.

They took their seats and were impressed by an array of meats and vegetables placed around cutlery and dishes that cost more than Jake had made the last two years combined. He grabbed a fork and eyeballed a thick piece of roast beef but Eva interrupted everyone with a subtle tapping of her fork on a crystal water glass to get their attention. He put his fork down as did she, folded her hands and began to say grace.

Jake looked at Ed and was intrigued that there was religion on the yacht and folded his hands out of respect to the good Lord. He wasn't much of a religious person and couldn't remember the last time he went to church which was the basis for his father calling him a sinner every chance he could. He listened to the woman say the lords pray in Polish out of respect for Cloudia, then reiterated it in English, then invited everyone to dig in.

He was hungry and with every fork full he thanked the Lord to himself that he was alive and had shelter and promised, that if he ever returned to Key West he would make an effort to pay his respects to the Lord at least once a month.

"Where was I" The Doctor asked, as Elliot came around the table and filled their wine glasses with a 1989 Pinot Noir.

He sat back in the large wing backed chair and remembered where he had left off with his story. For a moment he watched as Jake took a sip of his wine and looked at the red liquid, smelled it and approved the taste to his host. The Doctor recanted that he had just turned the lights on in the second subterranean room, while Ed reached over and loaded his plate with seconds. Jake looked at him in disgust but Ed rolled his eyes at him sending him a message to mind his own business.

He went on to explain to his audience of two that he couldn't believe his eye's at what he had stumbled on in that second room. It was the size of an auditorium that included a stage and a lectern at the front of the room. A twenty foot banner stretched across the stage that read "Alles fur Duetchland" had confused him at first as he walked down the aisle to take a closer look. In this room he noticed there were several flags of other countries on display including the United States, China, Japan and England. He knew what the banner meant since he had done some research on the Nazi party in the late fifties for a book report on the rise of the Third Reich. With all the war movies that came out after World War II most of the young boys were intrigued by German medals and he new "All for Germany" was the motto applied to the blades of uniform daggers worn by the SA, or Stormtroopers.

Ten desks on each side of the aisle that had telephones and a plaqared with a name of a county in Florida. Broward,

Ocala, Seminole and many others he had noticed as he walked around the desks opening drawers to see if there were any papers that would give him some information, but they were all empty. He stood there and looked around and wondered what had been going on here but couldn't find any clues to why Jonathan would point him to this place. It must have been locked for years he thought as he picked up one of the old rotary phones to see if there was a dial tone. It was dead as well. He sat down at one of the desks, looked up at the lights and wondered why the place had power, but no telephones.

He walked down the aisle and up the steps to the podium and stood there and stared out at the silent room of desks and scratched his head. He opened the middle drawer to the lectern and noticed a birthday card sitting in the middle. It had no envelope, just a birthday card. He picked it up and opened it and it said "Happy B-Day Deceive it looks like a duct and acts like a duct, then it's a". He said the answer out loud and looked at the rear of the room and notice a forced air vent with the fan moving slowly from air coming in. He jumped off the stage and went over to the air duct and pulled a desk closer so he could climb up and look inside. Shining the flashlight in the vent he could see a box. He pulled on the vent but it would not move. There were four screws holding it into the wall and without any tools would be impossible to remove. He remembered the nail clippers on his car key ring took them out and after an hour was able to remove the screws, then the vent fell to the ground and he finally retrieved the box.

It was the size of a cake box and sealed with tape. He shook it and something metal clanked around inside. Maybe it was some sort of treasure he thought as he fidgeted with the clippers to make a slit in the tape. He peeled it back and opened the box and looked inside with the flashlight. He was a disappointed to find five 35mm film canisters so he looked around the room to see if he had missed something but he hadn't. This was what Jonathan wanted him to find? What did it have to do with his life being in imminent danger?

He began to get paranoid and decided that it would be best to get out and head for his vehicle, take the film reels and have a closer look at them in the privacy of his own home. He also thought that it would be best to take some photos of the place before he left, and took his camera phone out and recorded the room. He put the vent back on the wall moved the desk back to its original position then grabbed the box and exited the room. He was alleviated to leave, but in the excitement of wanting to exit he forgot to turn the light off, went back down the flight of steps reached in and flicked the switch.

He was practically sprinting down the hall with the box in one arm and the flashlight moving from left to right as he came to the door that led to the barn. He stood by and listened if there was anyone in the barn, but heard no one and slid the lock. He grabbed the combination lock, closed the door and slapped it on and went up the steps into the barn. He looked at his watch. He was down in the underground bunker for over two hours and the sun would be coming up soon. It was twilight and the sky was beginning to get brighter as he exited the barn and walked to his SUV and set the box in the back seat and covered it with a blanket. He started the SUV and drove around the front to the driveway and down towards the road. He slowed down as he came over a hill and slammed on his brakes as he and a Stuart County Sheriffs car almost collided head on.

"What the hell is the God Damn hurry" the deputy said as he got out and slammed his car door.

"Sorry officer" he said as he got closer to the SUV. He looked in the back to see if the box was still covered.

"Step out of the vehicle, Sir" he asked.

"I'm sorry about this, I was just looking for my daughter" He said stuttering his words.

"She's out here drinking in that damn barn, how old is she" he asked.

"She's sixteen. Thought I'd take a look out here since this is where the kids hang out nowadays" he said.

"What she look like, we'll get some of the other Deputies to keep an eye out for her" he asked?

His phone rang and he excused himself to the officer and answered it. It was his wife Marilyn of twenty five years calling, worried that he had been gone all evening. She was yelling at him that he shouldn't be out late by himself and that he should be home. He wasn't even listening to her and had to think fast.

"She's home. OK honey I'll be home in a few. You tell her that she's grounded. OK Bye" he said as he hung up the phone.

"She's at home huh" the deputy asked?

"Yeah God damn kids. You can't chain them to anything anymore" he said with stupid smile on his face as the cop stared at him for a minute.

"You head on home now and make sure you give that girl what she got coming' and if you think she's out here again, give us a call" he said as he handed him a business card.

"Thank you. Deputy......... Jethro" he said as he looked at the card.

"My pleasure" he said as he walked back to his patrol car and moved it to the side to let him pass.

The Doctor went on to say that he never had been so scared of anything in his whole life because he had no idea what the hell was on the films, and had never lied to the police he thought as he sped towards I75 back the way he came. His phone rang several more times and it was his wife. She bitched him out for ten minutes and he apologized for hanging up on her, but she was only worried about him and angry that he was out at 5:30 in the morning and told her he would be home in an hour. After apologizing for twenty minutes on the phone he asked her to find the old film projector they used to watch movies on long ago.

After two more glasses of wine and some desserts, Elliot began to clear the table. Jake excused himself, got up, stretched and walked towards the humidor to pick out an expensive cigar for desert. The aroma was salivating as the door closed behind him and he picked a Cohiba he had read about in a magazine. He rolled the cigar in his hand and smelled the fine stick of tobacco as the others adjourned from the table to a couch area by the bar. He was intrigued by the Doctor as he watched them through the Smokey glass of the humidor as they all sat down, but he had no answers as to why he was involved or why he was here.

Winslow's story was interesting and Nazi call centers in the farm country of southern Florida weren't abundant but it wasn't enough to convince him that he had to stay on the yacht and listen to any more of the story. He was going to give him till the time he finished the cigar to explain why he was aboard this yacht or he would ask to be let off at the nearest port and be on his way back to Key West, hook up with Lisa and relocate to another country.

They were laughing as he walked out from the humidor and sat down next to Ed and immediately lit his cigar. He puffed on it and the Doctor nodded in approval of his choice and Jake thanked him for his hospitality. Elliot came by with a fresh bottle of wine and topped him off and Jake swirled the glass and took a drag from the cigar. It tasted exactly as he had read about and was amazed by their accuracy. He looked at the clock above the bar and it was 9:28 and figured it would take a half hour to smoke the cigar and by 10:00pm if he had no validity as to why he was brought into this situation, he was going to have to part ways with these people.

"Why do you think Jonathan wanted you to find the bunker" Ed asked the Doctor.

Jake thought that was a great question and the Doctor continued that when he finally got back to his mansion in West Palm he took the box into his study where he looked them over. Each reel had a different date as he took the tin canisters out and placed them in numeric order from 1939 to 1944. Elliot had prepared the projector and he loaded the film dated 1939 onto the reel and excused the butler so he could view the film in private but Marilyn had come to see how he was doing after being out all night.

He explained to her that he had some work to do and that he needed a couple of hours to view the films and needed some privacy. She asked him if everything was alright and he reassured her that it was and she closed the doors to the study and left him alone. They had been together for almost twenty six years and he could see she knew something was bothering him, but he needed to see what was on the films that were so important to Jonathan.

He dimmed the lights and turned the projector on and the grainy image from seventy years ago appeared on the screen. He focused the movie and it became clearer that it was a film by the Third Reich and in subtitles stated it was produced by Nazi Reichsmarschall Hermann Goring's SS film commission. Goring, the highest ranking officer along with Joseph Goebbles, the head of the SS had made it a point to document Hitler's speeches to the German population. However he could see as the film went on it was not of Adolph Hitler but a medical documentary highlighting the new Genealogical Section of the Race and Resettlement Office in occupied Poland. The narrator boasted that the brand new glistening facility would enable German scientists and doctors to expand their research into the effects of diseases on the human body as well as taking clinical science to a new level while experimenting on Jewish and Non-Jewish prisoners of Auschwitz, Dachau, Buchenwald and Mauthausen-Gusen concentration camps.

The narrator noted that all of the experimentations over the last several years had been documented meticulously and that all the information collected would be stored in a hall of archives. The heads of the research teams will be able to collaborate on their new findings to produce extremely effective results for producing deadlier biological and chemical weapons. All successful findings in the research facility would be dispatched to and reviewed by Goering,

Goebbels and Heinrich Himmler, head of the Schutzstaffel or SS. They gave all autonomy to their scientist in the three main concentration camps to perform any experiment in their field that they had wished and use as many subjects that they wanted to get the scientific results they needed.

Doctor Winslow was aware of the atrocities at the Nazi death camps but didn't know the extent of their research. Some of his colleagues who specialized in neurosurgery debated that if it were not for neuropathology's, Dr. Julius Hallevorden, director of the Kaiser-Wilhelm Institute of Brain Research in Berlin and his study of the many murdered psychiatric patients at Brandenberg, the understanding of child neurology would not be as advanced. Winslow pointed out to Jake and Ed that he was not an admirer of the scientists work but did agree some findings were essential in today's medical breakthroughs, but at a sacrifice to thousands if not hundreds of thousands of people.

As the 1939 movie reel on the new research facility came to an end Dr. Winslow was confused at what he was viewing. Being a leading researcher in the development of integrating micro computers into the spinal cords of paraplegics over the last fifteen years he had never heard of, or seen photos of such a place. For the next twelve hours he worked his way through the five more years of films and as a scientist he was intrigued, yet sickened by the morbidity of the Nazi doctor's research and development into diseases and viral outbreaks in a controlled setting. Most experiments he had read about were absolutely horrific acts of butcheries and dealt with the fascination of death and the many ways a person could die. The most notable responsible were Joseph Mengele, Carl Clauberg and Eduard Wirths whos experiments were so ghastly and sick to read about, yet even those deeds of injustice yielded scientific results but the Germans had a different agenda after they conquered the world. They were able to develop at least twenty five genetically engineered or mutated diseases they planned to unleash on the world and only pure aryans would have immunity towards. It was their ultimate final solution and the beginning of world domination including the destruction of their allies.

He put the movie reels back in the box and locked them in his safe and asked Elliot to prepare dinner for him and his wife by the pool. It was late and he was obligated to tell her where Jonathan had sent him so early in the morning and what he had found in the bunker but would spare her from viewing them. In the morning he would call on an old friend of his who had worked closely with Machek Strysewski a Biology Professor who helped form the underground education movement known as "The Secret Teaching Organization". The movement educated young Poles at Stefon Batory University in Wilno (now Vilnius) from 1939 to 1944. Education of the Polish under the Reich was banned and punishable by death. Many of the Professors that weren't taken to the concentration camps were able to work at German research facilities and had been exposed to the highest of "top secret" research.

Strysewski had worked at Plosnan University located on the Warta River in western Poland which is halfway between Berlin and Warsaw. With its vital rail networks during the war Ploznan was a major hub for Germany, which brought in supplies to be cataloged and reloaded on trains then routed to their destinations across Europe. He was responsible for shipments of medical supplies including

Cyklon-B that would eventually be distributed to the concentration camps within the Third Reich. Most if not all the documents on experimentation including specimens of body parts from the camps were sent to Berlin and had to be checked through Plosnan then loaded on trains to be studied and reviewed by Karl Genzken, Chief of Medical Office of the Waffen SS.

Winslow said he awakened early the next morning and called his friend Dr. Hans Sturmer whom he had met at a Endocrinology seminar at the University of Baylor in 1979. Sturmer was near eighty eight years old and still had a sharp recollection of the war, the German army and his friendship he had with Strysewski. It took several years for the doctors to become friends and sit down and talk about their lives and accomplishments in the world of science and as they conferred more often over the next twenty years he realised how entrenched he was in the documentation of scientific experiments. He claimed that he had not participated in any deaths of Poles or Jews, but was part of an eight man review board at the Race and Resettlement office in Berlin, that prioritised the studies for further research. Over the years he had developed a sense of compassion for Poles and their inability to be educated and by 1941 he and Strysewski had become friends and conversed on the phone on a regular basis. Sturmer was able to help the underground education movement with research documents and medical books that had been banned in Poland by the Nazis through a special code they had developed for communication. In turn Sturmer believed some good could come out of the war through science and education.

They talked on the phone for over ninety minutes. Winslow asked him if he knew of a facility in Poland that had been built sometime in 1939 for biological research such as creating and incubating diseases. In his line of questioning he didn't mention the films and the bunker he had come across in the past days and when Sturmer asked him why he wanted to know such a thing Winslow informed him that he read an article that there had been 335 infectious diseases dicovered or created since 1940.

It happened to be an article he had read also and wasn't quite sure if it had any corralation between Nazi experiments but noted that seventy five percent of those diseases had derived from the domestication of animals. Winslow pointed out that it still left under a hundred and twenty-five diseases that suddenly were among humans such as HIV and Ebola which don't have any cures and probably never will.

Sturmer explained to him that there were many documents that passed through his office. Some were sealed envelopes that were labled top secret and addressed to the Reichsfuher himself but those documents were handled by Genzken who met with Himmler on a regular basis. In regards to a secret lab, if there was such a place, his staff never knew of such a facility but he told the doctor that the Nazis were so secretive, anything could've been possible.

Before he hung up the phone, Sturmer had pointed out his views of the Doctors Trials at Nuremberg. He thought of the trials as a big joke and Winslow asked him why he had thought that. He reminded him that of the twenty three defendants twenty of them were doctors and one evaded capture, seven were acquitted, seven received death sentences and the remainder received sentences from ten years to life imprisonment. What was most appalling of the sentences was that they had been all commuted and released within five to seven years and continued working in the medical field until their deaths.

Some doctors, he continued, were even recruited by the United States Government and were subsequently alowed to continue their research. There was one doctor, he said had always stood out in his mind as being responsible for many deaths, but was spared the gallows, and that was Kurt Blome.

Blome, deputy of the Reich Health Leader studied cancer research at the Reich Research Council where he conducted experiments with plague vaccines on prisoners at the Dachau camp. Eventually, he would be arrested in 1945 by the United States Counter Intelligence Corps in Munich where his identity remained unknown for some time. He was then escorted to Kransberg Castle, north of Frankfurt after his true identity came to light then would be interogated by members of an Anglo-American team of experts who were investigating German and Italian advancements in weapons technology at the end of the war. Officially, on paper, he had been studying cancer research, in reality he was studying bacteriological warfare. In 1947 at the "Doctor's Trials" he was acqitted of conducting experiments on humans, which was made possible for his devulgance of his studies to the Anglo team in preparedness for their own germ warfare program.

Winslow had asked him if there was any account of diseases that had been manufactured during the war and Stumer told him that as the fall of the Reich was foreseeable by Goering. Documents were being burned around the clock until the Russians broke the doors down to the Reich's Chancellory. He then mentioned that it was the Americans that were more interested in German scientific studies, and that the Russians seemed not to care until it was too late. By then, most of the remaining documents had already been carted away, probably to Washington D.C. It was believed, that this incident was when the Cold War actually started and each side became increasingly decieving of their findings at other German Government facilities.

Jake had given him a few extra minutes to continue with the history lesson, but still wasn't sure what it had to do with him. He was intrigued by the Doctor's story and never heard or read of anything like it, but his patience was growing thinner by the minute. He had gone this far in listening and needed another beverage. He got up and walked over to the bar and poured a triple of vodka, leaned on the bar and decided to stop screwing around and asked Winslow why he was on this yacht.

"Yeah, I would like to know the same thing" Ed also asked?

"Don't get me wrong Doc, the story is great but why are WE here. Especially me. I'm just a bartender. No offense Ed" Jake said looking over his way.

'I understand. But if you bear with me, this will all make sense in a few moments' Winslow said, as Elliot came over to refill his wine glass.

He came from behind the bar sat down and looked at Eva. She smiled at him. Both women were stunningly beautiful and at that moment he realised that there was a international connection to the two of them and as they waited for the Doctor to continue. There was a greater importance to their role for being on the yacht. He felt it by looking at them and their attentiveness to the Doctor. Whatever had happened in their country years ago they were prepared to fight and die so that the story could be heard, and Doctor Winslow was their voice.

10:15PM

****

Johnson and Sinclair sat across from each other for the past ninety minutes and hadn't spoken a word since they boarded the plane. He could see in his friends face as he looked out the window that he was not happy to be heading to D.C. in the middle of the night. He wanted to break the ice and explain why there had been three of his men killed, a helicopter pilot and a building blown up while he was in charge of the Southern command center but his laptop lit up with an incoming video call from Maggie. He put the head phones on and answered it hoping it was good news.

"Talk to me girl" he said in an upbeat tone.

"Earnest Sniveley, Sir" she said.

"Who the hell is that" he asked looking over at Johnson to see if he was paying attention but excused himself and walked towards the restroom.

She informed him that Sniveley was the man responsible for the process of encapsulating information, whom she had met a few years ago at the data conference at Harvard, but he had been missing for over a year. He had an eventful life in the IT world and several run-ins with the feds and was linked to the "I Love You" virus from 2002 but was given clemency if he worked as an anylist for Homeland Security detecting source IP addresses from possible terrorist threats. Eventually he was let go after three years of good behavior and the assistance in capturing several high-level terrorists.

Sometime around 2006, she continued, he had become a Conspiracy theorist and was an on-line member of at least three chat rooms known to rant about the injustices that the Government was supposedly responsible for and became a respected leader in the chat rooms. It was in these chat rooms that he had been approached by another member where they became friends and corresponded in code that she couldn't break but was able to trace the screen name of the friend to an IP address from a coffee shop in Barbados back as far as late 2006. After that he dropped off the face of the earth.

"Who was the screen name" The Commander asked?

"Well that's where it gets tricky, Sir" She said.

She went on to outline the teams last few years of chasing Jonathan Pressley. The closest that they got to him in late 2006 was in Barbados but by the time the team had closed in on him he had disappeared as well. Sniveley's bank accounts had been closed and his parents hadn't heard from him in years. The parents had come to the conclusion that he had been murdered and would never be found but their bank accounts had been inflated over the years and were living modestly in Quincy, Massachusetts.

"Obviously Pressley had gotten to Sniveley" He said.

"Yes Sir, I also dug deeper into the parent's bank accounts and didn't find anything out of the ordinary. They invested, in what else, tech stocks and made a pretty penny" she said.

"Can we tap their computers for any communications" He asked?

"Tried that Sir, they don't even have cable television. Like I said there's nothing out of the ordinary. No cell phones, nothing" she said.

"Their son is still alive, they have to be communicating. Find out how" he said.

"Yes Sir. There's one more thing" She said.

Maggie also told him that she ran the prints from the van through Interpol and located where the FIM-92 was purchased. The prints came back to sisters Cloudia and Eva Turowski who are wanted for the bombing of a Cytogenic lab in Warsaw in 2005 that killed several scientists who were experimenting with the Black Plague and its effects on human tissue. It was presumed that their mother, a head researcher at the facility was killed before she was about to go public with unethical experiments on humans but was never proven. People believed she was murdered and the authorities concluded she died from blunt force trauma to the head from an automobile accident. The sisters were outraged that the investigation ended so quickly and believed their mother was going to expose two R&D facilities as well as a major pharmacuetical company for its testing and infecting of human subjects and after an attempt on their lives to keep them quiet, they took revenge by blowing up the lab.

While on the run, they were able to set up several web sites proclaiming injustices by the government and research facilities. They gained a large following of conspiracy theorists who donated money in support, but eventually they just dissapeared and their bank accounts in the Cayman Islands went dry and somehow Interpol hadn't heard their names until now.

"And the rocket" Sinclair asked?

"Yeah, that's a juicy one also" She said.

The FIM-92 along with fourty others were stolen from a NATO convoy that had been ambushed enroute to a French military command post outside Kabul, Afghanastan seven months ago. Thirty-two of them had been recovered from a storage facility in Miami after the ATF had raided the home of a suspected arms dealer from Germany named Helmut Schmidt. After a gun battle between the agents ended, they were unable to interrogate Schmidt since he had multiple bullet wounds and subsequently died at the scene. However, Schmidt happened to be a meticulous keeper of records and detailed the sale of three of the rockets to "One really hot woman" for thirty-five thousand dollars each.

"It had to be one of the sisters" Sinclair said.

"Yes Sir. I have both their pictures up on my screen, they are both exceptionally pretty" she said trying to make light of the situation.

"All right. Enough. We need to find out who's financing these people and email me photos of our latest subjects" he said.

He needed to be prepared he thought as he ended the video call with Maggie. Technology had exploded in the past ten years and he had forseen the future where super computers were being put in place to keep information on the public safe from the public. He held a conference with the Director of National Intelligence at the beginning of

2005 shortly after The Intillegence Reform and Terrorism Prevention Act was passed in late 2004. His posistion was created to oversee the US Intelligence Community thus taking away those duties away from the CIA. When this split happened the DNI formed a central database for the retention of records on every US citizen with a social security number. A person's life is digitally recorded to their file which is matched to their SS number and data such as spending habits, migration, doctor visits and credit card transactions is compiled for a profile on every citizen. The DNI anylizes the information to determine if a person is happy in his or her daily life, who's sad and who could be a possible threat to the government from this analysis.

In the meeting with the DNI, Sinclair, with his prior technology guru in tow, went to excruciating pains to inform him that implimenting such technology would eventually be breached and compiling data that could be accessable would compromise the integrity of many nations. The Director dismissed his analogy and stated that the people brought in to keep the information secure were the best in the world and that the amount the US government was paying the computer specialists, it would be almost impossible for anyone to get through. He tried to tell them that the advancement of technology would speed up at a rate that would be too fast to keep pace with but his boss Admiral Edward Faulk, Chairman of the Joint Chiefs of Staff, standing next to the DNI dismissed his claim as well. He left the meeting with the impression that they had it all under control but that wasn't case. Now he had supporting evidence that it was inevitable the project would be compromised.

Sinclair folded the laptop closed. Johnson sat back down and asked him point blank, what he was into. It was the first words that they had spoken and he hadn't prepared any answer that would make his life more meaningful. He sat back in his seat and looked over at Taylor. He was balled up on the chair as he had been on many other flights across the world, fast asleep. He decided that it might be best to explain some things to his friend.

The two of them had lost contact for the past several years and when he had learned of his wifes death he immediately checked to see if his children had been exposed, and fortunately they had been passed by in the process which didn't happen very often.

He sat back and explained the whole operation to Johnson from its inception sixty years to its purpose for present day. However, after an hour of listening it was obvious he was having a hard time comprehending that his wifes death had actually been a murder. He put his hands on his face and couldn't believe what he was hearing. Sinclair got up and walked over to his friend and touched him on the shoulder for comfort and reminded him of the oath he took to defend this country against its enemies foreign and domestic. Johnson wiped the tears away from his face and excused himself to the resroom. Sinclair thought he took it better than he expected as he watched his friend close the door to the restroom behind him.

He sat down and let out a sigh of relief. For the first time in twenty years he felt like shit for being a protector of the program. He viewed Johnson as a tough man, loyal to his uniform and a career soldier that would come out of this an even stronger officer if he got involved with the race to save the planet. The program could use a commander of his stature. He was in charge of J.A.I.D but was also second in command of USSOCSOUTH, Special Operations Command South located in Homestead which would give the Joint Chiefs of Staff a wider range of resurces. It was hard enough for the Department of Justice to acqiure new resources without exposing the program.

Johnson exited the restroom and stood in the isle of the plane next to Taylor. Sinclair could see that he was extremely agitated and his face was red with anger. He reached into Taylor's gear and grabbed his MP5 machine gun and turned it towards him. He closer and Siclair stood up from his seat and tried to get him to put the weapon down but he was irrational with a crazy look in his eyes and had every intent on killing him. He had seen it all to many times in a soldiers face and if he didn't do something the plane would go down for sure.

"Listen, this all happened before you met your wife. It's something that's not controllable and is needed" Sinclair said as he stepped a little closer.

"Do you have any idea the suffering she went through? It was the most horrible thing I had ever witnessed" He said as tears rolled down his cheeks.

He held the weapon high and told Sinclair to stay where he was and began to pan the weapon towards Taylor, but it was too late for Johnson to notice his attacker. He squeezed the trigger of the machine gun in fright, squirtting off three rounds. Taylor plunged the blade into his neck killing him instantly. Fortunately for them two bullets went into the restroom an the third imbedded next to the window cracking the first layer of glass but not causing any disruption to the flight.

"God dammit, Christ" he said as he ran over to his friend.

"He would've taken the plane down, Sir. I had no choice" he said remorsefuly.

"I could've talked to him" he said as he kneeled over his blood soaked friend

"Sir, It would've done no good. He was distrought. He would've killed all of us" Taylor said as he patted the Commander on the back.

He knew Taylor was right as he stood up and looked at the dead man who had endured many combat missions in Kososvo, three tours in Iraq and Commanded the relief effort for Hurricane Katrina victims. He was an exceptional soldier, father, and mentor to many people but this was the way of the world and to protect the stabalization of the planet for the future, more people would have to be sacrificed to achieve that goal.

10:40PM

****

Elliot came by with a tray of coffee and desserts as Winslow continued with his story. It was getting late and the excitement from the day was beginning to catch up with Jake as his eyes began to get tired. He opted for a coffee and some kind of pastry topped with chocolate figuring the sugar would perk him up. He was finding himself more interested in what the Doc was saying and wanted to know the purpose of the bunker he had discovered and its connection to the flash drive. Twenty five minutes ago he was ready to jump off the boat and swim to the nearest island, now he decided to listen to the man until he was finished.

The Doc continued with his story, that after his conversation with Strysewski, Marilyn had suggested that he contact the curator of German history at the Smithsonian and reports the bunker to the feds. It sounded like a good idea but came to the conclusion that it would be hard for him to explain how it had been discovered. He didn't know who Jonathan really was and where he had found this information, what secrets were behind the films and what connection they had to him but he made the decision to fly to Washington the next day and present the films to the curator anyway. He elected not to tell the feds about the bunker but was in a pickle on how he was going to explain to the museum where he had obtained them.

The next morning after packing his bags and a quick breakfast with his wife he placed the films in a metal briefcase, locked it and loaded the SUV. His private plane, a six seated Corsair would be waiting for him at Ft. Lauderdale International Airport for the solo flight to the Capital. Marilyn insisted that she come with him for company since it was such a long trip but told her it would be better if she stayed at home and not to worry and would return in a few days. She kissed him goodbye and drove down the long winding driveway and waited for the huge wrought iron gate to open. She had always worried about him when he flew alone.

He pulled out of the driveway looked in the mirror to see the gate closing behind him and headed for the freeway from his Fisher Island mansion. It was a forty-five minute drive to the airport once he crossed over the bridge into Miami Springs then on to I95. It was a beautiful day for flying he thought as he turned left onto the bridge and almost crashed into a dark blue car which skidded to a stop sideways, blocking him. Then suddenly, behind him a second dark blue vehicle screeched to a halt, blocking him in completely.

"Who were they" Ed asked?

"At this time I had no idea' "he said.

Two men jumped out of each vehicle pointing pistols and demanding for him to put his hands out of the SUV. He complied and they yanked him out of his car, handcuffed him and threw him in the back of one of the sedans. When he asked them what he was being arrested for, he was told to shut up. He glanced back through the rear window and noticed that they were driving his vehicle to wherever they were going. He had an idea that they weren't cops but was full blown military as he sat back in his seat and kept his mouth shut.

They drove up I95 through Biscayne Park and exited on route 924 and headed west for an hour into Opa Locka airport and pulled into an empty hanger at the end of the runway. He had been there before on a test flight for a plane he'd been interested in buying and hadn't change any in the ten years since. It was a small, out of date airport with one landing strip in the middle of nowhere that didn't even have a tower to spot planes landing.

They stopped the car and his captors yanked him out of the vehicle and walked him over to a single chair in front of a long table and sat him down. He asked them if they happened to know who he was and how powerful he was. They both looked at him and smiled while the other two men opened the trunk of his SUV and pulled out the metal case and placed it to the table. He looked at the case and then at his captors and wanted to know who the hell they were and what they wanted with the briefcase.

Off to the right of the hanger an office door opened and a man walked towards the table and sat down. He introduced himself as Commander Sinclair, with Navy intelligence and ordered the men to take the handcuffs off. He told Dr. Winslow that they were not going to harm him if he opened the case. All they wanted to know was how he knew about the bunker in Stuart and who told him to go there and then they would let him go, of course without the briefcase. He did what they asked and the Commander waved to one of his men who walked over to the case, squirted lighter fluid on the contents then lit it on fire. He hesitated with his answer as he sat back down on the chair and watched as history went up in flames. Just as the Third Reich had burned millions of literary publications these were going to be lost forever as well. He wanted to know one thing, would they harm him if he told them about Jonathan.

"I thought at this point I was safe to tell them who gave me the information" he said.

"Why did you think that" Jake asked?

His relationship with Jonathan was on a recreational basis. He admired the young man for his free will attitude towards life and his dedication to his work but up until the time he came to his home, they had never talked seriously about government issues or world problems but, over time, he did notice his demeanor change in their three year friendship. He had become more reclusive with his research at the Palos Alto lab and wouldn't be seen for days and producing enormous results. The letter had sat on his desk for several weeks because he had thought the young man had flipped out and went to great lengths to make him believe that his life was in danger. The bread crumb trail that led him to the bunker made him re-evaluate Jonathan's actions at the lab and he was now convinced that he was meddling in government information.

He agreed to give Jonathans name to the Commander. In return he would not speak of the films to anyone and let his team inspect the hard drives of the computers he was working with at the lab. It seemed harmless since he didn't know who the Commander was. He would let them dig as deep as they wanted. He couldn't afford to upset the Government when his funding for the project was under review.

Commander Sinclair walked the Doctor to his SUV and thanked him for his honesty and informed him that he would put in a good word with the Appropriations Committee to get his funding he needed. Sinclair leaned in the vehicle as he started it and apologized for the handcuffs, handed him a business card and asked him to call him if he hears from Jonathan any time in the future. Winslow shook his head in confirmation of the man's orders and drove back to his home and didn't mention the incident to anyone except Marilyn.

"How did the wife react when you came back and told her what happened" Ed wanted to know.

"She thought I was half way to DC by now" he laughed.

Marilyn thought that it was a good idea to distance them from Jonathan and reminded him that the funds from the Government were all too important for the research facility. If he didn't get them, it would cost millions of dollars to support and possibly ruin them financially. She knew he was interested in the films and wanted some explanation to all of it but was right. He had a business to run and twenty thousand mouths to feed so he agreed with her and eventually let it go.

Two months went by and the thought of the films and the bunker had passed. The research facility got a seventy-five million dollar grant, fifteen more than expected and the company was well on its way to making paraplegics walk again and advancing in other research as well. The board members were happy that the Doctor could secure such an enormous grant but he knew the Commander was the real reason behind its success. They got what they wanted and so did he, he thought.

As the weeks went by Jonathans name had almost slipped from memory until one day after a long round of golf, he opened his locker after showering. Somebody had left a cell phone on the top shelf. He picked it up and looked around to see if anyone had placed it there by mistake but no one was around. He dried off and began to get dressed when it started to vibrate. He looked at it and hesitated to answer it.

"Doc it's me. Don't hang up" The voice said as he flipped open the phone.

"Jonathan, is that you" he asked?

It was him and he told the Doc the phone was untraceable and that he was sure they had bugged his house in order to find out where he was. He whispered in the phone asking Jonathan why he had betrayed his trust by using his lab computers to hack into Government data and what was with the wild goose chase out to the country for the box of films. He raised his voice and told him that they came to the facility and they had looked through all of his hard drives for three days and left without saying a word.

"Because they didn't find anything Doc" he said laughing.

"Do you think this is some kind of joke, you little shit? I could've lost my funding" he said irately.

He told the Doc to calm down and asked him if thought he would still be in business if they had found anything.

The phone was silent. Jonathan apologized for bringing his facility under attack from the feds and that he only used his facility to further substantiate his findings. He stated that the reason for no evidence was that he used a virtual drive to save all of his information then exported it to a secure server away from his facility leaving no trace on the actual hard five its self. He reminded the Doc that he was smarter than they were.

Dr. Winslow looked around to see if anyone was listening but was still alone and asked Jonathan politely to not have any more contact with him or his family. Jonathan interrupted him and told him to stop being such a stubborn, snobbish bearcat and to look at the big picture and really think about what he had seen on the films. He reminded him with a stern voice of how much of a mentor he had been and admiration he had for his success but not to forget that his life was still in danger and time was running out.

"I'm in perfect health, Jonathan. I just had a physical. Now leave me alone." he said angrily.

"Get checked for pancreatic cancer Doc. Keep the phone handy. I'll call you in two weeks when you get your results" Jonathan said then hung up.

The guy was crazy he thought. He threw the phone in his bag and got dressed. Pancreatic cancer didn't run in his family and how would he know he had it he thought as he put his wallet in his pants when Commander Sinclair's card fell on the floor. He picked it up and started to dial the number but paused before he pressed the last number and sat down on the bench looking at it, wondering what to do. The right thing to do would be to call Sinclair and turn Jonathan in but deep down he wanted to know what it had all meant. He decided to call his doctor tomorrow and see if he did have the cancer Jonathan said and if he didn't, he would then turn him in to the Commander in two weeks.

'Well what do we know as of now' Dr. Winslow asked his guests.

"From what I knew of Jonathan, he was an interesting person. He was a hacker not a liar" Jake said.

'Exactly how I felt about him. Not once did he ever lie to me or my wife' he said.

Winslow concluded that he didn't mention to Marilyn about the contact he had with Jonathan knowing that the house was possibly bugged by the feds. He scheduled the test from the phone that was given to him and kept the conversation at home to a minimal. His physician said the test results would take several days and went home to wait for them patiently. He couldn't imagine that Sinclair's men had been in his home when he wasn't there and it infuriated him that they would invade his privacy. He wanted to call in an expert to rid the house of bugs but didn't want them to know he knew about them. They obviously thought they could do what ever they wanted.

Six days went by and his physician called and asked him to come to his office and needed to speak with him as soon as possible. Winslow had instructed his doctor to not say anything about his results over the phone and to keep it private from his wife as well. It had been a long wait and the drive to Miami Beach was stressful. He felt the news was not going to be good and Pancreatic cancer was dangerous but cureable if it was caught early. If had entered stage two, his odds were not good.

He walked in to the office and by the look on his face, it had been true. His doctor informed him as he sat on the cold examining table that he was in the first stages of the disease and would be treatable with lite chemotherapy that would be the end of it. His doctor mentioned that it was fortunate that he came in for the exam and Winslow told him it must have been his intuition. He scheduled an appointment for the chemo and went to his car where he sat for twenty minutes to absorb the results when suddenly, the phone rang. He was shaking as he reached for it. It couldn't be anyone else except Jonathan and answered it.

"For your sake Doc did they catch it early" Jonathan asked?

"How did you know" he asked?

"We have to meet. I'll be in touch with you after your chemo" he said and hung up the phone.

****

The jet touched down at Ronald Reagan International Airport and taxied to hanger 21 at the north end of the airport. Sinclair and Taylor covered Commander Johnson with a blanket and exited the plane as it stopped next to a black limousine. At the bottom of the steps awaited four men, two of them dressed in suits were from the Presidential cabinet and the others were from the Joint Chiefs of Staff. It had been the second time in the past ten years that political and military personnel together had met him on a tarmac. The first was shortly after the 9/11 terrorist attacks, and by the look on their faces, they werecertainly not happy.

The two sides were always at odds with each other on the purpose of the program. The military used it for controlling destablised governments where the politicians used it as a double standard for saving humanity and the planet by limiting humanity on the planet. However on both sides, over the years, they agreed that it had been hard to recruit people from different influential sectors in both of their professions and the demise of Commander Johnson it would leave a gap in their surveilence over the four corners of the United States. Standard operating procedure mandated that if an individual was not with the program then there was no reason to continue the courtship and secure the information and then they would be terminated.

Sinclair put his emotions to the side as he came to the bottom of the steps and walked towards his two superiors, Chairman of the Joint Chiefs of Staff Admiral Donald Babbitt and Chiefs of Staff of the United States Army, General Micheal McDonald. He stopped in front of them and soluted them and reluctantly informed them that Commander Johnson would not be joining them for the meeting and that they had disposed of him due to his unwillingness to participate in the program. They looked perplexed as they glanced over at the politicians who began whispering to each other while glaring at the Commander.

Being a career military man he had never been a big supporter of politics and over the years his disdain for them had grown. His budget had been cut and the recruitment of civilian personnel into the program had diminished in the past several years. He knew it had been harder for them to allocate money after they computerized the tracking system under the ruse of the Y2K scare and the financing of two wars. However, he had warned them that the old days had gone long ago and the program would eventually become harder to conceal. Now as they were about to take a ride to the White House he had hoped that they all had a plan to stop the inevitable.

****

Dr. Winslow had kept the attention of his two guests and continued with his story. The cancer was at the early stages but surgery would have to be done on the pancreatic head, followed by chemotherapy. It had been an agonizing ordeal and after two months he had been named the luckiest man alive and his chance for survival was almost a hundred percent. He had done a lot of soul searching over the past several weeks. As the days went by and he got better he couldn't wait to hear from Jonathan and to thank him for saving his life and to find out how he knew he had the disease.

He had been released from his doctors care and was allowed to continue with his travels. Marylin decided after this ordeal it would be nice if they took a vacation to Isla Mujeres, a small island north of Cancun, Mexico to get away from the city and the research facility. The next day they flew the small Corsair across the gulf, landing in Cancun International Airport and took a taxi to the Port of Jaurez for a jet ferry to the quaint little island. They packed lite for the fifteen day stay and booked a room at hotel Na Balam, a quiet hotel on the North beach where the rooms had no televisions and the tiki bars were within a stones throw. It would be perfect for relaxation he thought as the the jet ferry roared towards the island, he wondered when he would get that phone call from the man that saved his life.

They unpacked their belongings and settled into the room and by the fifth day, the low key vacation was everything they needed. It had been a week since he left the care of his physician and he hadn't heard from Jonathan. He checked the phone regularly for missed calls, but on the sixth day things changed when he was sitting on the north beach reading a book. It was like a market place with vendors walking past with offerings of raw coconuts to hand crafted jewelry and even frozen icecream in the scorching sand. It had gotten somewhat annoying in the past day for Marilyn so she decided to sit by the pool for a different atmosphere and some caribbean music.

It was a beautiful cloudless morning and the view from the white powdered beach was captivating as he watched the small boats take tourists out for diving and fishing across the waveless water. It was almost ten in the morning and his doctor had advised him not to drink, but he was in the mood for a large margarita to start the day off right. He decided to walk the fifty yards to the nearest tiki bar and took a seat at one of the swings around the beach bar and waited for the bartender who was flirtting with two American tourists girls.

After two minutes of getting no where he eventually came over and introduced himself as Jose, the greatest bartender in Mexico and took his drink order. He claimed to be the greatest but from what he had seen he was the slowest and the most unkept bartender he had ever seen with greasy hair and dirty fingernails. Standing at five-two he could hardly see over the bar, but since most of the natives were Mayan Indians no taller than him, he wondered why they had built it so tall.

Jose set the enormous margarita in front of him and the Doc gave him a ten dollar tip so that he would remember him later. Jose thanked him gratiously and asked him his name and he told him who he was. He looked surprised and waved for him to come back to the bar. He called him over to the end of the bar and told him that a man had given him an envelope yesterday and a thousand pesos to make sure it was delivered to Doctor Winslow. He looked around but there were only a few people on the beach this early in the morning. He opened it and read it.

> Doc,
>
> Glad to see you've recovered well. It is time we have a little talk.
>
> Noon tomorrow, you and the wife take the ferry back to Cancun. Cab # 53 will be waiting. Pedro a friend of mine will be your driver. He drives really fast.
>
> Take in a bull fight at Plaza Del Toros at 2pm.
>
> See you then
>
> J.P.

He thanked Jose, put the note in his swim trunks and walked back to his beach chair with his margarita. For some reason Jonathan hadn't called him. Had they followed him to Mexico he thought as he looked around at some of the people nearest to him. No one looked suspicious as he looked over every one. He needed to get rid of the note just in case. He ducked in to the restroom and flushed it down the toilet. If he had been followed, no one, for sure, would know where he was going tomorrow.

"Did you feel like you were being followed" Jake asked?

"Well, I started to observe a lot more, let me put it to you that way" he replied.

He looked at every one for the remainder of the day and fidgeted during dinner. Marilyn asked him if everything was ok and he told her that he would enjoy taking the noon ferry to Cancun to see a little bit of the city. She took a bite of her steak and looked him over for a few seconds and then agreed that it would be a good idea to get off the island for a day. Paranoia had set in and he mentioned nothing of the note or the rendezvous with Jonathan. He remembered the house had been bugged and they could be listening to every word they said. Besides, it was Jonathan who had followed him to Mexico and it was time to get some answers.

11:15PM

****

They entered the limo for the ride to the White House Situation Room to debrief the President and several other highly paid politicians about how out of control the situation has become. They took their seats directly across from their superiors and off to the left sat the two suits looking perplexed, holding their briefcases in their laps. Sinclair knew the one on the left as National Security Adviser David Turner but did not know who the young man that accompanied him.

Admiral Babbitt took the liberty of introducing him as Lawrence Dobson, the newly appointed Chief Technology Officer to the President or more preferably known as the Internet Czar and newest member of the team. Sinclair had been informed some weeks ago that a new person would be acquired but paid little attention to the memo, looking briefly over his credentials and who had recruited him.

Raised in Newell, West Virginia, a small coal mining town across the Ohio River, Dobson found his calling in computers at a young age and was eventually awarded a full scholarship to Stanford University at seventeen. At twenty-one he was lauded by the Pentagon for his success in voice and facial recognition software that was implemented as the main identification program for security clearance in most of the high level government facility's including the White House. At twenty-four years old, he had been recruited by the Department of Defense and dubbed the most dangerous computer whiz in the country.

His career moved into high gear after the newly elected President, the youngest ever, had to have him on his team. Not only was Dobson smart but the new Commander in Chief thought he brought an appeal to the younger generation by being a roll model for the future students of technology and educating for a new era where rival countries would eventually depend on the United States for goods and services.

Babbitt recruited him several months into his new post with an offer that his family would be taken care of physically and financially and accepted without hesitation. Sinclair didn't care who he was and what he was capable of accomplishing. The program was in jeopardy and the information had been compromised and as far as he was concerned it would take a thousand computer geniouses to stop these hackers and the people who wanted to expose the government.

"What the hell happened in Key West, Commander" Turner asked?

"You mean the ten thousand things that have been happening in the last two years. Don't you Turner" he replied as he leaned into him.

"What he's trying to say Commander is Do you think it is stoppable" General McDonald said as he put his hand toward Turner to calm him down.

"I've been developing..." Dobson started to say when Sinclair interuppted him.

He explained to the young man that their resources had been tapped and restricted. If it were not for the two daughters of a well respected Polish doctor who worked for one of the Cytogenics lab that had been eliminated a few years earlier. The mother had decyphered codes in four prenatal medications and the process of who would receive them. They both looked confused and he went on to explain who they were.

The two girls had sworn revenge after their mother had left them a detailed diary of her involvement in the manufacturing and dispersement of diseases across the globe and her constant fear for her life. Two days after the H.I.T.S team was dispatched to her, the Cytogenics lab burned to the ground. The two sisters were seen on video firebombing the site and hadn't been heard from until earlier this evening when a finger print found on a FIM 92 rocket was used in Key West to take down one of their Choppers had been a confirmed match to one of the sisters.

"What are you saying Commander, two women are responsible for the Keys disaster" Turner asked?

"No, what he's saying is the two are well funded. Rockets like that aren't cheap Turner" General McDonald said.

"We're thinking they have an endless supply of cash" Sergent Taylor said.

"Explain to me how you came to this conclusion" Turner barked.

The Admiral and the General, who had been his superiors for several years, would have agreed with him fifteen years ago that the program should've been the sole responsibility of the military. They had gotten old and complacent, and obviously ready to retire any day. They did their time and should have been replaced with a younger generation who had more balls to stand their ground when it came to protecting the integrity of the program. However, the Government was running the show and had over extended themselves as usual with two wars and the meddling in every other countries business. It was people like Turner, who hadn't lifted a finger in their whole life. He had been in politics for years and assumed everything was going well and that the data bases would never be hacked. It was all about votes and keeping their jobs and somewhere along the way they lost sight of one of the most secretive operations, that, if uncovered would propel the word into mass chaos.

"Weapons, passports and high-tech computers don't come cheap" Sinclair said.

"They've gotten really high tech. We believe they've recruited some highly skilled individuals who have been able to do things we haven't seen before" Taylor said.

"How could this happen gentlemen? Post 9/11 created an infrastructure that was unreachable" Dobson said.

Sinclair sat back and gazed out the window looking at the Washington Monument in the distance as they turned right on NW Pennsylvania Avenue. They were less than five minutes from the White House where the President, the Secretary of State and the leaders of the ten nations that support the program were about to get a wakeup call.

If Dobson was the smartest man on the planet he thought, maybe he could put an end to this nightmare.

****

Dr. Winslow said that he and his wife awoke early and enjoyed the continental breakfast then walked the beach to the 11:00am ferry. Marilyn had come across some advertisements for some local clothing shops that she wanted to visit and buy a hand crafted rug for the patio. He agreed with her as they boarded the jet ferry to Cancun but knew Jonathan would have other plans for them. By the end of the day's excursion to the main land, she would be furious with him that she didn't get to purchase the rug.

There were several other people taking the mid day trip to Cancun and no one looked out of the ordinary as they sat on the upper deck to get some fresh air. A young couple sat across from them holding hands as the huge jet engines roared and the large catamaran took off, sliceing north through the ocean. He noticed there was a family of four on the lower deck and an old mayan man sitting in the corner with his belongings pled around him. He must have seemed uneasy as Marilyn grabbed his hand and assured him it would be over in twenty minutes. She didn't know that it wasn't the boat trip that made him edgy, it was the meeting with Jonathan and the thought of her being harmed that bothered him. He smiled at her and gave her a kiss on the cheek and she smiled back.

Twenty minutes later, the catamaran came to a stop at Port of Jaurez. They disembarked towards the terminal and walked passed a MacDonalds and a taco stand, through the exit where the taxis staged for fares. He steered Marilyn towards cab #53 that was sitting off to the right of the treminal where Pedro was waiting with the door ajar. As they got closer a driver of another cab grabbed his arm and tried to persuade them to get into his cab. Pedro walked over quickly and intervined. He and the other cabby yelled at each other for a few seconds, but eventually he was able to lead them to his vehicle.

They climbed in the small four door and he introduced himself as Pedro. He closed the door and walked around to the drivers side, had several more words with the other taxi driver then got behind the wheel and took off. He advised them to fasten their seat belts and Marilyn looked at him surprised. They took his advise as they sped across the Bonampak Highway towards the city at a high rate of speed. She instructed him to drive to the shops at La Alhambra but the Doctor told her to relax for a minute. She gave him a puzzled look.

"Give me the cell phone, Doctor" Pedro said.

"What cellphone" Marilyn asked.

"It's ok honey" he said as he reached into his shorts and handed Pedro the phone that Jonathan had given him.

He took the phone and continued to speed along Bonampak Highway looking in the rearview mirror to see if they had been followed. He told them that the phone Jonathan had given him was bugged by someone who had been in his room two days ago and they were probably tracking it through satellite as they spoke. They stopped at the circle and cut across to Kaan Chac and turned left on a cobble stone street lined with food concesionairs. That didn't stop Pedro from speeding through the crowd and skidding to stop then turning right and then left down winding roads through the city.

Marilyn was terrified and Pedro was apologetic for his driving but assured her that it was necessary. She asked him if he was going to harm them and he smiled, revealing a full set of gold teeth and told her that he was not the one whom she should be affraid. She then turned to her husband and looked for him to do something but all he could do was ask that he slow down so they didin't kill anyone. He smiled in the rear view mirror and obliged.

They drove a few more miles through backroads of impoverished neighborhoods and stopped in front of a cantina where Pedro got out and walked up to an old man who was sleeping in front of the bar. He put the cell phone in the mans pocket of his poncho, came back to the car and sped off down the road laughing. Ten minutes later they came to a stop in front of the Plaza del Toros where he let them out and told them to enjoy the show.

"How much for the taxi" The Doc asked him and Marilyn looked at him as if surprised that he would pay for that hellish ride to near death.

"Put your money away Senore. I just hope you join us in this fight" Pedro said as he got back in his car and sped off.

They walked towards the entrance to the arena and Marilyn demanded that he tell her what was going on and why he had been associating with Jonathan Pressley. He grabbed her hand and pulled her toward the gate and quietly told her that it was Jonathan that told him he had the prostate cancer and if it were not for him he would be dead. She wanted to know more but he hushed her as they came to the ticket window, purchased two seats and were informed that the next fight would start in fifteen minutes.

As they walked down the corridor to the arena, he explained to her that he didn't have a lot of information about what was going on but informed her they were to meet Jonathan at 1:00pm. He assured her he would give them the answers to all of their questions and to be patient. She didn't say a word as they came out of the tunnel but he knew she was furious with him for being involved with Jonathan again but he didn't care what she thought. He was alive and if Jonathan knew he was to die soon, how many others did Jonathan know about.

He was amazed at the size of the place and upon entering the arena the crowd cheered as a man on horseback displayed his lassoing talents. There were also numerous people in colorful outfits dancing around celebrating the Spanish and Mayan culture and entertaining the locals as well as tourists who filled the arena almost to capacity. It was large enough and more modern looking than he had pictured from the outside. He admired the architecture. It reminded him of the Dallas Cowboys stadium, but only a little smaller.

They walked up the isle for a close seat. The bottom five rows of the arena had comfortable cushioned seats but were taken by the locals. They continued towards the top section and sat down on the second to the last row which was occupied by mostly young tourist vacationing and partying on their parents' credit cards and taking advantage of the drinking age in Mexico. The seats were cement. Not what either of them had anticipated as Marilyn shot a frustrated look at him. He told her that they shouldn't be there long enough for them to be uncomfortable.

The crowd cheered as the announcer asked if there were any Americans that were willing to test their bravado in the ring with a juvenile bull and a young man off to the right, jumped up, climbed over the rail and took his place in the ring. His friends cheered for him as the band struck up a paso doble or spirited bullring march as they dressed him in a maroon Curro Romero gold embroidered jacket and a red capote to ward off the bull.

They were amused as well as the locals at the sight of the young man being tossed around while trying to fend off his aggressor. He had not been a match for the juvenile bull but was cheered as he left the arena and took his seat. He was disheveled and a little embarrassed as some of the locals came by to throw jabs at him. He smiled and laughed as his friend's poked fun at him as well.

The opened dome ceiling gave no relief from the heat as the first fight began and he could feel Marylyn was already uncomfortable as she fidgeted in her seat. They had never been to a bullfight in their worldly travels and the first sword that went into the bulls shoulder blade made them both whince as the crowd cheered wildly for the bullfighter. It was ghastly, with blood squirting from the bull. Marylin had her right hand over her face and was squeezing his right arm with the other when he heard a familiar voice from behind.

"Glad to see you two made it" the voice said.

"What the hell" he said as he turned around.

"You know, you two stand out like a sore thumb in here" he said laughing.

They both turned around and looked at Jonathan but didn't recognise him. He had grown a full beard and donned a sombrero to fit in with the locals. He looked as if he hadn't taken a shower in a week and from his offensive body odor, Maryilyn would have guessed two weeks as she distanced herself from him. His disguise was impecable as he stood up and cheered for the Matador as he put another sword through the bull then sat back down and gave them his undevided attention.

"It's been a pretty wild couple months for you both, huh Doc, and I'm sure you two have a million questions" he said.

"I don't care what things you may be into young man. All I want to say to you is thank you for saving my husbands life. Thank you and God bless you" she said touching his hand.

They were both taken aback by her kindness. The Doc would have bet a million dollars that she would've torn into him and then stormed from the arena. At that moment he saw a different dimeanor in his wife that was alleviating and exciting to him as she had realised the importance of this man. He couldn't wait till they got more answers to the conundrum that had been place before them and finally shed some light on the events of the last three months.

It was evident in his voice that the Doc was angry that they had been followed to Mexico. More so, he wanted to know how they had been able to do so.

Jonathan explained they had tracked him through his GPS from the black box on his plane, as he did. He knew they would corner him in the hopes the two of them would either turn him in or draw him out for capture. He had been wise to their game and their resourses were very scace in Mexico since the election of a new president and almost all participation in the program had been put on hold. The American government had not been too popular in Central America. Since they delared war on Iraq, less money had been flowing their way and in turn more politcians were not getting thier pockets lined.

11:25PM

The door to the Situation Room opened and President Conrad Fullerton walked in. The first African-American to be elected Commander in Chief, had been a junior Senator at best. Only in office approximately eleven months he had very little accomplishments on his record and mostly spent his days talking on the phone with foreign dignitaries and giving speeches to colleges about overcoming the fear to succeed.

His campaign focused much on a promise that every American would be able to have health insurance under his National Care Act, which appealed to most voters and subsequently got him elected. He was a movie star to people and mesmerized them with his charm and gorgious wife Sarah and their two children Claire and Kate. The people cheered for him as if they were the Kennedys, but the reality of politics was going to change him forever.

"Good evening gentlemen" the President said, as he sat down.

The men stood up soluted him then sat back down. The majority of them were unsure how they felt about their new Commander, especially Sinclair. This was his fifth President that he had to sit with and explain the details of this highly secretive project. Sinclair could recall only one President whom had an issue with the project and that happened to be John F. Kennedy and his fate was sealed in Dallas in 1963 for wanting to expose the truth and it was Sinclairs father who had orchestrated the assassination.

"Admiral Babbitt, what is the meaning of this late night meeting" the President asked?

"Commander Sinclair will explain everything to you Sir" the Admiral responded.

Sinclair stood up and over the next sixty minutes, explained in detail of the project that all the men in the room were responsible for. From its inception in 1943, to all the modifications that had been made as technology grew over the years. He explained the purpose, how it works, who is involved and why it has to be protected, but most of all he explained, that it was imperative that the United States President has to give his full cooperation and attention to this matter.

After listening intently President Fullerton sat back in his chair. It was a lot to chew on and he was visibly shaken by this news and wanted to know if his family had been infected, but Turner informed him that they all had been immunized immediately after he had taken office.

The look on his face was in disbelief and was sick to his stomach at the thought of all the people who had died over the last seventy years, including his family members. He sat up and asked Sinclair and the others what would happen if he was to not be a part of the program.

"Well Mr. President, look at what happened to JFK" Turner said.

"You'll... I'll need a minute to think about this" the President said nervously.

The President paced back and forth for ten minutes. He had been thinking hard about this situation. If it were exposed it could quite possibly cause a global civil war and he wasn't going to go down as the man responsible for that.

He came back to the table and leaned into his men and explained to them that he was in and that they had his full cooperation. They were to contain the problem or dismantle the project and he was to be kept informed at all times, of what was going on.

"Gentlemen, I'm in let's making this happen or it's all our asses" the President said as he walked out of the room slamming the door behind him.

"That went better than expected" Dobson said.

"Yeah, but let's see if he keeps his mouth shut" Sinclair said.

Admiral Babbitt told his men that he has absolute confidence in the President. Do what he asks and make sure he is kept informed, and if he doesn't cooperate they will have no other option than to eliminate the man and his family.

"Ok men lets head to the Pentagon, you all know what to do. Let's make this happen" Babbitt said as they all walked out the door.

Sinclair got into the limo with Babbitt and Turner. The mood was somber and even though the Pentagon was a short ride, it seemed like hours. He was glad the President was on board, but the next twelve hours were going to be crucial. They still had the hacked information. Soon they were going to expose themselves. Either way, he felt it all slipping away.

All the work over the years and all the deaths made him tired and wished it was all over.

****

"Now here's the juicy part" the Doc said with excitement.

Finally, Jake thought. He was tired and getting a little drunk while listening to this man. He was facinating and had an outstanding way of telling stories. His hand gestures and voice sometimes roaring but mostly soft spoken was captivating. Jake understood why people had missed him dearly when had disappeared several years ago.

He continued that they moved from the Plaza del Toros to a small taqueria around the corner called Restaurant Labna. Jonathan had become friends with the owner when he informed him he was in the early stages of kidney cancer. After the discovery, the owner Jorge Estaban welcomed Jonathan with open arms every time he arrived.

"Welcome, welcome" Jorge said as he walked them to a secluded room in the back.

They introduced themselves and Jorge gave them each a big hug and said that they were blessed to know such a man. They both agreed and sat down at the table, ordered margaritas and munched on some chips and pico de gallo.

"Now, what I'm about to tell you is going to seem really farfetched, but listen and bear with me" Jonathan said

It all began September 1, 1939 with the invasion of Poland. Hitler didn't want to invade but he needed a crucial part of Poland that would make his plans to conquer the world move faster, and that was Poznan University. It was located half way between Warsaw and Berlin and he wanted it but the leaders of Poland would not let him have it. This infuriated Hitler and took it anyway.

"World War II was started over a University" Marylyn asked.

"Yep, not just a University, Poznan University" He replied.

Poznan University of Medical Science was started in 1919. It was the first University in Europe with a pharmaceutical department and in 1939 the Germans had to have it. After the invasion of Poland the doors to the University were closed. Many of the teacher's especially Medical Science faculty was allowed to stay on with their respective departments. Many had little choice in the matter.

But by 1942, he continued, the war was in full swing and U.S Army intelligence had been receiving reports that people were being experimented on by Nazi doctors. America was not in the war yet but was concerned by the information its spies had been transmitting. By midsummer the U.S had critical documentation that German doctors at several of the Polish concentration camps were engaging in and creating major diseases that could be dormant in DNA and awake at any given moment. Test kits were manufactured in Poznan then delivered to the concentration camps where they were then injected into endless amount of human subjects killing millions of people. All tests kit studies were very well documented by the doctors.

"You mean the Germans mapped DNA in the 40's" the Doc asked.

"Yes sir" Jonathan replied.

But by the end of 1942 America's hands were tied. It became increasingly harder to get into the labs, and dozens of spies were murdered. The United States needed to get into the war and the Bombing of Pearl Harbor was the catalyst they needed. They declared War on Germany as well as Japan.

"Doesn't that seem a little convenient Doc" he asked as Jorge and a waiter brought them plates full of food.

"A little too convenient" the Doc. said

The Office of Strategic Service, now the CIA was commissioned to spearhead the move to obtain the documentation on the kits from the camps. Their intelligence told them that all findings by the Doctors were meticulously recorded, boxed and taken to the Reich Chancellery building in Berlin and stored in the Fuherbunker, Hitler's massive underground bunker. They would be stored and then used for the "Final Solution" after Hitler took over the world.

"What kind of findings" he asked Jonathan?

"Plagues, viruses, cancers. Things of that nature" he said

By 1945 the race was on to get to Berlin, unfortunately the U.S wasn't the only ones in the game. The Russians had been leaked some information about Biological weapons being stored in Berlin

As well. Stalin, by then had proven to the U.S and England that he was a certified nut bag and it was futile that the United States Army make it to Berlin before they did. The OSS (US) was not going to allow that to happen. They sent out hints of false information over a two week period claiming all important files will be moved to the Reichstag. Stalin's men intercepted some classified documents and under scrutiny had his men turn toward the Reichstag building. Both of his Generals opposed Stalin's idea but turned their attention to the Reichstag, making it their first stop.

"They went to the wrong building" the Doc said laughing.

"They did but I somehow wish I they hadn't" Jonathan said.

By the time Stalin and his military realized that there was no hidden stash of biological weapons they rushed over to the Chencellery, and as they were walking in the front door, the United States Army was walking out the back with truckloads of boxes nicely packed and heading for Fort Detrick, Maryland.

Ft. Detrick became the main research facility for the United States' biological weapons program. It opened in 1943 and lasted until 1969. The facility supplied the world with contaminated vaccines, but today it's mainly used as an underground storage facility.

"If I understand you correctly, you are implying the Government, OUR government, is responsible for my cancer "the doc asked astonished?

"Correct, I did say distribution" he said.

"How is this possible "Marylyn asked?

It was not only cancer but other diseases such as influenza. As a trial run the project sent vaccines loaded with the flu to Africa in 1947. Ultimately it killed 40,000 people one year later. It took them a few years to get the project up and running. There had been massive amounts of papers to sort through. The Nazi's infected several million people with a wide variety of diseases and choosing the ones that would be most lucrative in the future was a daunting task. Then, by 1950 the government had dubbed the project Operation

Population Control and by 1952 they had partnered with the three biggest pharmaceutical companies in the world. By 1980, those partnerships had mainly become silent and the U.S government was in total control.

That year in 1980, was a turning point for the project. Thirty years had gone by. They changed the name to Human Integrity Protocol and in 1981 they launched a full blown A.I.D.S epidemic in Africa that rapidly spread to the United States, claiming millions of lives. It became a business for the HIP. They gained more silent partners like hospitals and added nine countries like China who agreed they had lost control of their population by the late 1970's and were desperate for help.

"It's population control" the Doc asked.

"Yes, and big business for Hospitals" Jonathan replied.

By 2010 sixty percent of the baby boomers were sick with some kind of chronic disease and Hospitals had become so big they put their IPO's on the stock exchange selling in sick. Medications were being handed out like candy and the "business" turned from killing, to prolonging death so everyone makes more money. No one is exempt, not even rich people. The Pharm companies, Hospitals and even the funeral homes only care about making money. The project was so secretive they have their own Task Force called HITS, the Human Integrity Tactical Squad; they are the protectors of their Holy Grail.

"Get the hell outta here Doc" Jaked said laughing.

"That's really unbelievable" Ed said

They had evolved, the Doc continued. The bunker he had entered was the first stages of the project. Several underground facilities like the one he had been in were built across the country and housed doctors from Germany and the Nazi party to extend their research. Housed in fully operational labs they were able to developed some of the most dangerous biological weapons ever made, but eventually those facilities became obsolete and by 1960 the doctors had vanished and the bunkers, were left behind.

By mid 1950's dispersement came in the form of a simple shot that was mandatory, like polio vaccine, to infect certain areas of the country. In those shots that people received would be Leukemia, maybe a stronger strain of the flu, and could take several years to make people sick. Those shots were given to people of any age, in the hospital, even newborns.

As technology advanced in the 70's a person's social security number became the prime way to distribute the diseases. By the time you are one year old you will have several shots and the ninth digit determined what you will be infected with. If the last digit of your Social security number is 6, many years later, you will be the host of some kind of cancer. The only number that does not receive a virus is the number seven.

"That same system is still being use today" the Doc said

"Wow Doc that's some deep shit" Jake said

"Where are these vaccines made" Ed asked?

There have been millions of the vaccines made, the Doctor continued, and is currently being stored at a distributing facility outside of Washington DC, called River City Logistics. It's a one man operation and the only employee, probably has no idea what's in the orders he fills all day, and Hospitals all over the world order directly from that company. It was a front for H.I.S and has enough supply of the vaccines to last them a hundred years and have no need to make more. Unfortunately, only 120 million antidotes were made for most types of infections and are being kept secured in an underground facility outside of Fort Detrick.

"You're saying 120 million antidotes but there could be a thousand for a certain disease and a 100k for another, correct" "Jake asked confused.

"Precisely what I'm saying" the Doc responded.

"We need to go there and get that shit, my number ends in 3. So what do I have" Ed asked with a look of dismay.

The Doc had Elliot show everyone to their quarters, and advised them to get cleaned up and get a few hours sleep. The Doc said in a couple of hours a helicopter is coming to get them and take them to the island of Saba in the southern Caribbean. There they would all find out what fate had been issued to them, and if they're prepared to take action against H.I.S. and the governments responsible. He had the plan to make it happen and it wasn't going to be easy.

12:20AM

****

H.I.S. headquarters was located twelve floors below the Pentagon. Originally a deep impact bunker when built in 1941, it was converted to a high- tech information technology police group in 1990 and used to compile data on every citizen in the world. The facility had several functions. First, it was the brain behind the program and responsible for dispensing the infected vaccines to the hospitals through social security numbers, Secondly, it kept massive amounts of data on victim's life progress including trips to the hospital and ultimately their death.

The facility was the first line of defense for cyber warfare. All internet traffic was filtered through H.I.S. headquarters before it was diverted two floors up to the Department of Defense. Cyber techs look for hackers and people that use key words that may alert them to possible intrusion into the data bases. The staff of 50 was the best hackers on the planet and was working franticly to find a shred of useful information

"No one leaves until we find these people" he said as he slammed open the door to his headquarters.

Sinclair took his place at the bridge, an elevated area that gave home a 360 degree view of the room. He was glad to be back he thought as Maggie came running over to him. She looked disheveled with a stack of papers in her arms as she welcomed her boss back and informed him that everything was a good to go.

"Nothing is going to get through this time Sir, I can assure you of that" Maggie said.

"Did you get that Stanley Dobson situated" he asked

"I did Sir and boy is that guy a genius" she replied.

Dobson was across the room typing franticly. Maggie explained that he had come up with a formula that could break past a senders IP address and reveal, down to a one square mile a person's location, even if the IP was 16 bit encrypted.

"That's great" Sinclair said shaking his head as if he had understood what she was talking about.

He walked over to his office where Turner and Admiral Babbitt had been on the phone with the President for the past ninety minutes bringing him up to pace with the situation. Turner rubbed his eyes and looked as if he had his brain scrambled.

"The President is a tough person to explain things to" the Admiral said.

"You do have a failsafe plan, Commander" Turner asked?

He did have a failsafe plan, but it was not the option that he wanted to use.

In 1999 he was authorized by the President at the time to install twelve Electro Magnetic Pulse devices all over the world. These EMP's were so powerful that the world would be taken back to the dark ages, if used. When activated the magnetic pulse would destroy anything with electrical parts and circuit boards, thus rendering it useless forever. This final solution was not what he wanted but if cornered he would have no choice but to use it.

****

He opened his eyes and it felt as if he had just closed them as he was awakened by the sound of a helicopter landing on the bow of the yacht. He was rested and slept as well as he could but was still tired from the past days ordeal.

There was a knock at the door, Jake opened it and it was Dr. Winslow. He invited him in and took a seat on the edge of the bed and began to explain that there had been a change in plans and asked him if he had any objections to breaking into Ft. Detrick to retrieve samples of the antidotes.

Jake sat down in a chair across from him and took a deep breath. It wouldn't be any different from Iraq or Afghanistan except that it would be ten times, if not twenty times more guarded than any Taliban compound he had raided.

"I know your background Jake. This was why Jonathan wanted you with us" he said

"That's a tall order Doc. Why" Jake asked?

"Marylyn is sick. She is in bad shape with breast cancer and needs a cure and that cure is at Detrick" he said eyes watering.

The Doc explained to him that he would not be going just for his wife but it would be a humanitarian mission to acquire the medicines and bring them back so that more could be made, and when this secret is exposed to the people of the world, there will be a huge need for cure the human race.

He was right. Someone would need to break into Detrick and steal at least one cure for each disease in case they would be destroyed. He would need help and it would not be an easy mission.

"I got a small team standing by in Bermuda, Eva is going as well and your friend Ed will go to Sabo with us. We will need him there" the Doc said smiling as he shook his hand.

"I'll do it. It's not going to be easy" Jake said.

"Thank you so" Winslow said as he grabbed him, pulled him close and gave him a hug.

Jake was flattered the Doc had thought of him that way. He informed him that they would call Lisa and let her know he was alive when they reached the Island. Jake thanked him again and promised that he would not let him down and grabbed some things and headed to the chopper where Eva was waiting. They both boarded and waived as it took off for the Island of Bermuda.

04:30AM

Ed, Claudia and the Doc were ready as the second helicopter was making its landing on the bow to take them to Saba. Winslow instructed Elliott to take the yacht to Puerto Rico and he will radio him when it's all safe, and for them to pray.

The trip to Saba would take about three hours and by then the Docs ace in the hole, Earnest Sniveley, the best hacker in the world will have their system up and running and ready to take the blindfold off of the world.

4:40AM

She hadn't said to much the whole trip. Only that the men he was going with were some of the best fighters she has known and to put his trust in them. She was sweet and nice and made him feel comfortable about the mission.

"We will be landing in two minutes" the pilot said

"Roger that" Eva replied.

The chopper touched down on Somerset Island, the old port and landing strip for the Royal Canadian Navy back in the seventies. It was run down and since the Navy had abandoned it in the mid 90's it was the perfect place to launch a covert operation.

The pilot of the jet was hurrying Jake, tapping his watch as he went directly from the chopper up the steps and into the Leer jet where he was greeted by three men. They introduced themselves as Sgt. Sumner, Lt. Brian Bennett, and Capt. Don Nelson all former Delta Squad and familiar with Ft. Detrick's landscape.

"We've heard of you Jones, it's a pleasure" Lt. Bennett said as he threw Jake a duffle bag filled with gear.

"Let's Go, Lets go Gentlemen, we got a schedule to keep" the Pilot said as he walked down the aisle towards the cockpit.

"That's Paul Greely, Winslow's longtime friend" Eva said

"Greely, the man that broke the land speed record in 1988" Jake said.

"That's him" Capt. Nelson said laughing.

Greeley jammed the throttle and the plane accelerated fast as it left the small runway. They were airborne, banking towards Virginia. Captain Greeley addressed his passengers on the P.A and told them they should be there before sunrise which was at 7:10am.

"800 miles to Ft. Detrick, We should be there by six am" Lt. Bennett said.

"That's plenty of darkness for a night jump" Sgt. Sumner said laughing.

Eva laid out the plan. Greeley would get them as close as possible under ten thousand feet, about seven hundred yards from the North West gate where they will have to jump. The pilot will make a fake distress call to Dulles Airport which will allow them to evade the possibility of getting shot down. Making that call to Dulles should deactivate a code red situation and they should not engage the plane.

"Hopefully the jump doesn't kill us" Jake said.

"Or they shoot us down with a S.A.M." Lt. Bennett said.

"Even if the plane gets shot down, you guys should be on the ground by then" Eva said.

Once they were on the ground they were to follow the N.W. parameter fence for five-hundred yards till they reach Restoration Spring, a small pond in the rear of St. Josephs Villa, the site where the antidotes are being stored. The Villa was used for entertaining purposes years ago and now the basement is a locked down-fortified storage facility, guarded by five to ten armed guards around the clock.

"How do we get in" Sumner asked?

The Villa, built in 1895 on the top of the hill overlooking the pond was a Colonial masterpiece taken over by the Government and converted into Ft. Detricks command post for most of the cold war. The sprawling landmark had an enormous wine cellar and through that was the secret door which led several hundred feet down the hill to Restoration pond. The steel sewer pipe at the edge of the pond would be their entrance point.

"Another sewer" Jake said.

They all looked at him. He shook his head as Eva continued.

They would then have to breach the lid to the enormous pipe without setting off the entry alarm, which Capt. Nelson would take care of. Then proceed down the tunnel, by-pass the alarm system then blow the steel door and take out the guards in the converted wine cellar. After they gathered enough of the antidote samples they were to make their way to the main floor, take out the remaining guards if necessary head to the garage where there will be a vehicle, and drive out the North West gate, which should be guarded by two guards.

"Yeah we're a little familiar with all of this" Bennett said.

"You want us to drive right out the gate" Sumner said.

"Man, that's ballsy" Jake said looking at the guys with his brows rose.

"Jake, if you are as good as they say you are, these guys will have no problem helping you get this done" Eva said.

When they were out the gate they were to follow 270 souths to a town called Clarksburg, but before they reached the town looks for a billboard on the left. After that billboard they would then take the first street to the left and follow it about two miles to a farmhouse on the right. In the barn, their transportation back to Bermuda would be waiting.

"If everything were to go as planned we should be in and out in less than thirty minutes." Bennett said.

****

Winslow, Ed, and Claudia were swinging around the south side of the Island of Saba, a small volcanic island located in the Caribbean Sea. It was a hidden paradise and its location gave him easy access to International Submarine Communications Cable. These cables, specifically the Americas-1 South cable is responsible for transmitting data from North America to Asia and Europe, and the main splice that connects all the countries was less than a mile from the islands shore.

"There's Snively he will catch you up to speed" the Doc said, as the helicopter landed.

Ed had heard of Earnest Snively through some of his computer friends. Supposedly, he was the sole man responsible for the Northeast blackout of 2003. Ed had also heard that he was declared dead as of 2009, but obviously that was not true.

"We're patched in Doc. We are ready to go. All I need is the flash-drive" Snively said as they were getting off the helicopter.

They walked across the heli-pad to a walkway that led down to a small mud-stucco building at the base of the volcano. Snively introduced himself to Ed and began to explain the procedure he was about to attempt using the undersea cables. They were going to force a Trojan virus that took Snively six years to make down the throat of the D.O.D and the H.I.T.S team. When they try to block it they will unlock a Worm that will take over their system and open the front door for them to broadcast all the information.

"What exactly are we broadcasting" Ed asked.

"The data on the flash-drive" Snively responded.

The flash-drive has every persons information who had been deliberately infected over the past fifty years, and in two parts they will transmit that information to every device on the network, like cell phones, laptops, tablets and any device that is using an I.P address. Then the final blow will be that all the data from the flash-drive will then be sent to every news network in the world.

"Asia and Europe won't be hard to break through, but the U.S will be exceptionally tricky" Snively said.

"From what I hear, you're the best hacker out there" Ed said

"Lawrence Dobson. He may be the best" Snively replied.

"They'll be waiting for us to transmit" Winslow said.

The mud-stucco building was one big open room with three computers and monitors. Snively took control of the main computer which was ready to go, and instructed Ed to sit at the computer next to him. He instructed Ed to hit "Enter" on his command.

Snively inserted the flash-drive into the computer and instructed Doctor Winslow and Claudia to sit down, and that they were making him nervous as he hammered on the keyboard.

"Here we go fellas" he said as the disk drives closed.

****

"Eight minutes to the drop zone" Greeley voice came over the speakers

"Gear up boys" Lt. Bennett said.

They were equipped with light body armor, MP5 sub machine guns with silencers and three grenades each. Eva came around to check each man, wished them luck and reminded them why they were taking this mission on.

"Two minutes" Greely yelled.

Their air speed was about 350mph when Eva opened the side door and counted down. It was going to be a rough jump as he looked over Sumners shoulder. He could hear Greeley putting out the distress signal to Dulles International Airport.

"Go. Go. Go." Eva yelled

Jake was the last to jump out the door. The wind caught him and flipped him over and just missed the rear wing of the jet. He was falling fast and having a hard time reaching his rip cord, but finally got his finger on it and pulled. The chute came out and he leveled off around four thousand feet. He could see in the distance the Jet banking south towards Dulles. Greeley and Eva were safe.

He tucked and rolled as he hit the ground, getting tied up in his chute. Sumner came over and helped him get unhooked and they rallied with the other two behind a barn a hundred yards away. They landed in a perfect location, approximately a half mile from their entry point.

"Everyone ok" Bennett asked?

"We got fifty minutes till sun-up" Nelson said.

They moved quickly towards the North fence and followed it until they reached Restoration Spring. Lt. Bennett had them stop and removed a spray can from Sumners backpack, took the lid off, covered his mouth and sprayed a large half-moon on the steel fence. The steel melted like butter and the half-moon of chain link fell into the grass.

"Won't that trigger a parameter alarm" Jake asked?

"It fuses the steel and fools the sensors into thinking everything's Ok" Bennett replied.

They crawled through the opening without touching any part of the fence, and moved around toward the enormous sewer pipe. The heavy lid which opened vertically had a sophisticated digital combination lock that Nelson got to work on. He removed the outer casing exposing some wires that he connected his test clips to and inserted the other end into the USB port in his mini laptop, punched in a few keys and the lock popped open.

Sumner flipped the lid open and went in first. Jake went next and following him was Bennett, then Nelson closed the lid to the entrance. It was pitch black and the team turned on their flashlights under their MP5's and made their way seventy five yards down the tunnel to the entrance of the storage facility. The door was locked, but Bennett pulled out a small block of C4 explosives and packed a small amount in the key hole of the door.

"Won't that make a lot of noise" Jake whispered?

"Not this amount" Bennett replied.

He put a detonator into the half-dollar size bit of explosive, waived the men back and counted to three. The explosion was soft and sounded like a book falling on the floor. Jake was the lead man through the door after it popped. The soldier sitting at the desk was up on his feet and reaching for his weapon when Jake pumped two rounds into his chest then swung around to take out the other soldier before he made it to the stairwell.

"Nice work Jones" Bennett said.

Jake didn't think it was nice work. He had enough of death during his military career, but managed to get off a smile as he and Nelson secured the area and retrieved the keys to the cold storage room. He tossed them to Bennett and opened it. Jake walked to the entrance where he joined the others who were looking into the long corridor in amazement. The corridor looked like a banks safety deposit room and the boxes that contained the antidotes had locks that required finger prints to open them.

"Fuck a Duck" Nelson said.

"You two go upstairs and wake the General, and bring him down here" Bennett said.

Bennett pointed at Sumner and Jake and they double timed it up the stairs through the door to the main floor. Jake took out the first guard who was sleeping at a desk and Sumner took out the second guard, who was making coffee in the kitchen.

They made their way to the second floor and turned left down the hall when suddenly Sumner put his hand up ordering Jake to stop. The general was awake and was in the bathroom brushing his teeth. They agreed that he would take the hallway entrance and Sumner would take the bedroom entrance to the bathroom.

They simultaneously entered the bathroom, but the General reached for the pistol on the counter, turned and pointed it at Jake. Sumner put two rounds in his head spraying brain and blood on Jakes face. The General fell and hit the tile, sliding to a stop at Jakes feet.

"What the fuck" Jake said.

"We aren't here to negotiate. Remember" Sumner said.

Sumner kicked the gun away, bent over the General and flipped him on his back. He sat the man up against the wall and grabbed his right hand and pulled out a twelve inch knife from the sheath on his hip and cut off both the Generals hands. Sumner turned to Jake and threw the man's left hand to him and laughed.

"Need a hand" Sumner said.

"Jesus" Jake said as he caught the hand.

The two had been gone for less than five minutes when they arrived back at the storage corridor. Bennett looked at them confused as they came down the steps and asked them where the General was.

"Have a hand Sir" Sumner said as he handed Bennett a hand.

"You guys are sick" Bennett said laughing

"Here's the other" Jake said.

"Good, you brought both hands" Nelson said.

There were a hundred and ninety boxes but fortunately one hundred-seven only needed to be opened. The Lieutenant and Nelson took the liberty of marking each box with a black "X" that had the antidotes that needed to be taken with them. After seven minutes the Generals hand print had opened all the boxes.

Jake took two viles of each antidote and put them into his backpack and the team headed upstairs where Bennett took a handful of C4, smashed it to the wall and equipped it with a remote detonator. He armed the bomb and ordered the team to the garage.

In the garage was a jacked up Jeep 4x4 with mud tires and a lift kit with the keys in the ignition. Jake started the motor and liked what he heard. Everyone climbed in and he hit the garage button and made their way towards the main entrance. It was 6:45 and the Fort was still sleeping as they rolled slowly towards the North West gate where a young Private stood guard.

"Is the General with you sir" the young man asked as he leaned into the window

"No but he wanted you to have this" Sumner said as he handed the Private the Generals hand from the back seat.

"What the F...." the kid said

"Open the gate" Jake said as he pointed the MP5 at the guard.

The Private pushed the button and the gate slowly opened. Jakes heart was racing a hundred miles an hour when the other guard a Captain, came out of the latrine and began to walk toward the jeep but Sumner shot him in the neck. Bennett smashed the button on the detonator and the Generals house blew into a million pieces as they peeled out of the gate. The young guard reached for his weapon and Nelson shot the young man through the rear window as they sped off down the road towards I270.

6:40AM

****

The virus and worm were ready to launch. This was their last chance to expose the governments and it had to work or they would be hunted and murdered like many others before them. People like Jonathan Pressley and hundreds before him were finally going to get retribution and show the world the truth.

Sniveley was excited as he made some finishing touches. He looked at all three of them and with his fingers pointing at them he counted down and hit the enter key on his computer and then instructed Ed to do the same.

"Well folks, here it goes" Sniveley said as he sat back in his chair.

The flash-drive was interacting with the network and the information on them followed the worm and the virus to its target. All they could do is sit and wait till the programs did their job and hope they were more powerful than the previous ones.

"What do we do now" Ed asked.

"We sit and wait, just like before" Claudia said.

"It's going to work" Sniveley insisted.

"It has too. We are running out of options" Winslow said.

****

"We got activity" Dobson said as he stood up.

"Find where there at" Sinclair said.

Maggie told Dobson to try and triangulate their location, but he said he was having trouble. They were being blocked by a virus that he had never seen before. It was taking over their computers and opening up the gateway. Their firewall was collapsing.

"It's going down" Maggie said

"We can't block them. They are taking over the internet" Dobson said anxiously.

The Commander paced back and forth deciding what to do, when suddenly the two steel doors to the room exploded open. Sgt. Taylor turned to fire but was taken down by two quick burst. Sinclair ran for the EMP button, but before he was able to press it, was shot in the right shoulder, sending him reeling to the ground four feet away.

The room flooded with Police, Homeland Security and the FBI. They ordered everyone to the ground including Admiral Babbitt and General McDonald, who came out of the conference room demanding an explanation for this intrusion when. To their surprise, President Fullerton walked through the smoke and ordered everyone in the room to lie on the ground.

"Do you have any idea what you are doing" Sinclair asked as he was being handcuffed?

"Yes. Yes I do. I am protecting the people of the United States, including my family" Fullerton said.

"You're dead. Fucking dead Fullerton" General McDonald said as all of them were being hand cuffed and walked out the door.

****

It was 7:05 and the sun was coming up. Winslow stood up and walked to the window and looked out at the ocean. It should have worked by now he thought when all of a sudden Sniveleys and the Doctors cell phone buzzed with notifications. He looked at the text message, showed the phone to the Doc and started screaming for joy at the top of his lungs. Doc Winslow looked at his phone and read the message to Ed and Claudia.

It said: You are infected by your government
Do not panic. Tune into any news channel
in the next 24hours with instructions to be
Inoculated. Please do not panic. We will
Cure you.

"You did it kid" Winslow said as he jumped and hugged all three of them.

"It worked. Holy crap" Ed said.

****

They made the hard left from Ft. Detrick to I270 and Jake jammed down on the gas pedal. They were two miles from the farm house when Nelson informed them that they had company behind them and told Jake to step on it. He looked at the side mirror and the vehicle was getting closer.

They made the sharp turn after the billboard and sped down the dirt road towards the farm house.

"Let me out here" Bennett said.

He jumped out of the Jeep and ducked into the corn field. He could hear the vehicle getting closer on the dirt road and pulled the pins on two grenades and waited. Timing it perfectly as the military vehicle went by he threw them into the driver window and before they knew what had happened the vehicle exploded into a ball of flames and came to a stop in a ditch.

Bennett hustled to the barn where the others had the door open and was pushing a helicopter out into the open. They opened the back door and began to climb in but there was a metal briefcase on the seat and handed it to Bennett. He opened it and inside was a large amount of cash and a cell phone.

"Let's get this bird in the air" Bennett said as he took the phone and put it in his pocket.

"What's the money for" Jake asked?

"I think it's for you Jake" Sumner said.

Nelson started the engine as they got in and buckled up. They were climbing off the ground and out in the distance he could see the home at Ft Detrick burning. Jake scanned to the left and noticed three more vehicles coming down the main road but they were good and clear as they banked to the right and headed for the coast.

"Damn that was close "Jake said.

"Yeah that was" Nelson replied.

The phone in Bennett's pocket began ringing. He answered it and began laughing and told everyone that Snively and the Doc did it and it was over. He talked with

Winslow for several minutes and informed him that he got all the antidotes as instructed and the mission was a success.

"You all did a great job. I thank everyone" he said as Bennett put him on speaker phone.

"Thank you Sir' they all said.

Bennett handed Jake the phone and Winslow thanked him and told him that the fifty thousand was for him and when they arrived back in Bermuda, Greeley would take him back to Key West where he could resume his life in paradise. Jake smiled and ended the call. The ordeal was finally over.

Two hours later the helicopter landed in Bermuda where Greeley was waiting next to the Leer Jet to take him back to the Keys. The men disembarked the plane and changed into their civilian clothes and congratulated each other on a mission well done when Bennett came up to him and handed him his cell phone and thanked him for coming along.

"You had that all along" Jake asked.

"Yeah didn't know if I could trust you with it" he replied.

"Tell your men to take care" Jake said as he walked over to the jet.

He boarded and sat down in the rear, flipped open the phone and dialed Lisa's number. She answered and when she heard his voice screamed with excitement. She calmed down and told her that it's all over and would be home in a few hours. He had a lot to tell her.

TWENTY-FOUR HOURS LATER

Twenty-four hours had passed. It was seven in the morning. Jake rolled over in bed, kissed Lisa on the forehead and turned the television on to the news network. It was the story of the decade and the media had already taken its steps to solve the problem and exploit the people involved all at the same time.

President Fullerton's cabinet was reeling from this catastrophe. Already making his speech in front of the Lincoln Memorial, he had an explanation and denied that he had anything to do with the program, but the public held him responsible for what happened until an old friend stepped in to shed a little light on the downfall of the Human Integrity Squad.

Doctor Winslow was now a worldwide star. He was the International man of mystery, and it would be him, a man who had disappeared to save humanity that would convince the people that they were no longer in harm's way. He would get his message through to them by standing with the government of the United States, the President and promising the people a healthy future and providing everyone with an antidote for their affliction.

It was all touching to Jake and in the end, life would go on. After all the demonstrations and rioting things would eventually get back to normal. The antidotes were going to be distributed in less than a month by Dr. Winslow. Fullerton built Ed a new computer shop. Eva and Cloudia started their own fashion business specializing in female military gear and Jake, his life was good he thought as he turned off the television.

The End

About the Author

Charles is originally from Youngstown, Ohio, but later

moved to Cleveland in the mid 90s and became a bartender. By 1999, he was sick of winters and intrigued by Tom Cruise in the movie Cocktailand Leonardo DiCaprio in The Beach. He didn't want to move to New York or Thailand, so he settled for the sandy beaches of Key West, where he bartended for many years. In 2008, he decided to return to Ohio and met his fiancée, Agnieszka, in 2009, and together, they have a beautiful boy who will be six next year. Besides mixing drinks, Charles has a passion for cooking and strives to teach his son everything he has learned such as to not be selfish and to be nice to everyone, no matter who they are.

Printed in the United States
By Bookmasters